I0570843

Ominous – A Collection of Dark Tales
Ian J. Middleton

ISBN: 978-0-473-52990-1

A big thank you for the help and support I received from the following people:

Kat Lilly

Denver Grenell

Adam Sherratt

Katherine James

Hopefully one day I can express my gratitude in more ways than putting your name at the front of a book.

Cover design by:

www.garthdesigncompany.com

Email: mike@garthdesigncompany.com

Instagram: @garthdesignco

Dig

You didn't need to be fluent in Russian to work out that the campsite was closed. The multiple signs that Tony cycled past—whether they were hammered into tree trunks or propped up against dilapidated fence posts—all implied the same frustrating message.

The dirt road he'd been following for the past half-hour came to an abrupt end at a moss-covered gate. Beyond was a grassy area about the size of a football pitch. Ageing trees lined the perimeter, their branches intertwining to form a thick canopy that would provide shelter from all but the heaviest of downpours.

Tony leant his touring bicycle against a clump of thick bushes and inspected yet another sign. A black silhouette of a tent sat within a crudely drawn circle with a scribbled line through it. A jumble of letters and shapes—indecipherable to anyone not versed in the local language—spelt out the symbol of denial.

A depressed sigh escaped Tony's lips as he once again regretted the frugal purchase of the out-of-date guidebook. It had been a several kilometre freewheel on his fully-laden bike to get here, and his body ached in protest at the thought of riding back up that road in search of another place to camp for the night.

The gate was inspected; a shiny padlock and chain reinforced the sentiment of the signs. The gleaming metal seemed so out of place in this backward area of rolling countryside. Over the past few days he'd passed horses dragging overfilled carts, weary farmers harvesting with scythes and oxen ploughing fields. He never thought he would miss the sight of asphalt, but the crumbling potholed roads were taking their toll on his body, bike and patience.

Tony looked back at the hill he'd just rolled down; it seemed bigger from down here. Further investigation confirmed that there were no farmhouses around or other signs of civilisation.

Deep in thought, he ran a grubby hand through long hair that was due for a trim several months ago. A glance at the darkening skies served to reinforce his unlawful intentions. With a shrug, the panniers were unclipped from the bike and slung over the gate. He glanced over his trusty steed; it appeared weak and naked without the stuffed bags attached to it. The red frame was scuffed and scratched, the tyres balding, and the improvised flag pole that once waved the Union Jack flag so proudly was drooping to the point that it would soon snap again.

The bike was lifted over the gate with a grunt. The bags were reattached and his belongings were wheeled to the far corner of the field. If he was going to spend the night, then it was in his interest to be inconspicuous about it.

Several mounds of earth were passed as he crossed the campsite. While some were in various stages of reclamation by Mother Nature, others appeared as though they had been dug yesterday. It was as if someone was searching for a lost artefact. He made a mental note to be away by sunrise, therefore mitigating the chances of being spotted by whoever was doing the digging.

The bike was propped up against a tree and camping gear unpacked. A tiny one man tent was erected and he was devouring a meal of packet noodles and cheese as the last of the daylight bled from the sky. Unless the weather was bad or the mozzies were out in force, he rarely ate within the tent. It was like a coffin in there. The compact and lightweight design came at the expense of having to sleep in it. Before he embarked on the world tour he would not have considered himself claustrophobic, but each consecutive night spent within the canvas confines forced him to reconsider that position.

The cooking equipment was packed away in the dark. The head torch remained in the pannier for risk of alerting his presence to any passers-by. He may have been in the middle of nowhere, but there was no need to tempt fate. As a result, he was forced into an early night. It wasn't necessarily a bad thing. The past few months of cycling across Europe had created a kind of deep fatigue that never really went away. While he was touring through the Eastern Bloc the bicycle had felt heavier, despite no additional items being added. Upon entering Russia he noticed that the bike required more and more effort to keep it moving in a straight line, as though the chain was coated in thick grease and the tyres were deflated. He could not remember a time when his legs didn't ache. He had expected to harden up to the six to eight hours of daily cycling, but the opposite seemed to be true.

Maybe he wasn't eating enough.

Maybe he wasn't getting enough sleep.

Maybe he was just over the hours of solitude, the weary body and constant nights in a cramped tent. He promised himself that once he made it to the next town he would check into a hotel, the only requirements being that there was a bath and a bed. The thought of the impending comfort brought a smile to his face and he buried himself further into the sleeping bag. His head rested upon an inflated plastic pillow and he drifted off to sleep.

**

A mechanical hum stirred Tony from his slumber. A check of the watch indicated that it was one-thirty. He'd not overslept, it was still dark outside. It took several moments to realise that it was a car engine that woke him. The opening and slamming of a door confirmed it. The vehicle must have already been at the locked gate, idling while the padlock was opened. As if to reaffirm Tony's suspicions, a clatter of chains landed in a heap on the ground. The creak of age-old hinges invited the car to proceed. The glow of the visitor's headlights was visible through the tent's thin walls. It seemed as though they were sticking to the other side of the campsite; that fact did not stop his muscles from tensing. The stuffy air within his cramped world suddenly felt colder. An anxious sickness deep within his gut began to churn.

The vehicle continued to roll forward and after a few seconds came to a stop. The engine was killed, snuffing out the headlights.

A door was opened again. The rustle of footsteps. A voice spoke in a language Tony did not understand. Another voice sniggered. There were at least two of them. Both men by the sounds of it. The accent suggested that they were locals of the Motherland.

Something clicked and the squashy compression of hydraulic pistons could be heard. Tony suspected it was the boot of the car opening. A hollow twang of metal on metal gave the impression that a collection of tools were being gathered up. A loud clatter soon followed as the items were dropped onto the grass.

From within a confined tent nestled away in the corner of the field, the lone tourist stared up at the taut canvas stretched several inches above his head, struggling to work out what was unfolding. The items sounded like gardening equipment, shovels, pickaxes and the like. If they were here to dig, why do it at night?

More indecipherable words were exchanged then a new sound joined the mysterious night-time gathering. It was as though a third person was also there, but their mouth was gagged or taped shut. A series of moans, desperate and pleading, filled the night air.

A muted thud silenced the stifled lamentation. A frantic shuffling soon followed, accompanied by the sound of laughter. Something was dragged across the ground. The muffled pleas intensified.

A single-worded demand was made by one of the men.

Tony was certain that the third person was now sobbing. The thought caused a flurry of goosebumps to ripple across his skin.

The demand was made again, this time more forceful. "Ko-pat."

An item was collected up off the ground and promptly thrown back down.

"Ko-pat."

The sobbing subsided.

There was a brief pause.

Then the digging began. The unmistakable sound of metal plunging into the earth and the spoils tossed to the side. The action was slow, the process drawn out.

Tony's eyes widened as he pieced together the audible clues. The sickness he felt when the vehicle arrived had increased exponentially. The tent started to swirl. The sides, already mere inches from his shaking body, began to close in. He racked his memory attempting to picture what was beyond the campsite. If he was to try and escape, what would he be running into? More fields? A forest? He couldn't be sure.

He eyed the entrance to the tent, the triangular zipped opening that would need to be negotiated without arousing suspicion. The tent was so narrow that there was no way he could turn around without causing it to shake from side to side. The rustling of the sleeping bag fabric sounded like the crushing of a car to his now hypersensitive hearing. He would have to bend himself double, unzip the flap and then shimmy out feet first. If he was lucky enough not to be spotted then he could dash through the trees and... and... what? Continue running barefoot, dressed in a t-shirt and boxers, until he reached the nearest village and explain through hand actions and gestures what he thought had occurred at the closed campsite? No, he would have to wait, and hope.

A check of the watch indicated that it was one forty-five. While he processed the limited options available, the sedate digging continued. The sobbing was now reduced to a quiet whimper, not unlike the restrained grief at a funeral.

The grinding of a lighter sparking into life occasionally joined the sound of shovelling, the two masters leisurely passing the time while they waited.

All Tony could do was lie there and listen to a condemned man dig his own grave. The areas of freshly disturbed soil he passed while crossing the grassy field now took on a new meaning. This was no campsite.

The time was rechecked: Two-twenty. At this rate they would be here until morning. A rush of cold swept over Tony's tensed body at the realisation that if that were the case, there was no doubt that he would be spotted. In a moment of selfishness he wished for the unfortunate individual to get it over with. There was no need for an innocent tourist to get drawn into... into whatever this was.

For some reason, Tony's mind drifted to the stories he had read of the Rwandan genocide, when the Hutus, armed with machetes, turned on the Tutsis. In one such horrific incident, a congregation was attacked. The church was barricaded shut and the armed militants slayed all who were trapped inside. However, hate-fuelled adrenaline only lasted for so long, and the aggressors paused midway to catch their breath. Drenched in the blood of their victims, they smoked cigarettes and rested, unaffected by the destruction around them. The wailing and pleading of all who remained went ignored. After a few torturous minutes the cigarettes were flicked away and the massacre continued. Tony was drowning in that same sense of helplessness now, with each passing minute that crept closer to dawn.

Another check of the watch: Three thirty-five.

The excavating noise was rhythmical, if at a dawdling tempo. Tony could picture it in his mind's eye.

The plunging of hardened metal into the ground.

The stomp of a boot on the blade.

The prising up of disturbed soil.

The tossing of soil up onto the grass.

Repeat. Repeat. Repeat.

Tony wondered how deep the grave must have been by now. How long did it take grave diggers to dig a six-foot hole? A couple of hours maybe. All he knew was that he didn't have long before the night commenced its retreat and the birds began to sing. On many occasions during the trip the dawn chorus was used as an alarm clock. It was a serene way to start the day, and so in keeping with nature; sleeping outdoors, travelling via pedal power and escaping the cities. But now that once beautiful sound hung over Tony like the Horns of Jericho.

At ten past four, the masters broke their silence. Something abrupt was muttered. It was impossible to know whether the required dimensions of the grave had been met, or they had simply grown bored. Whatever the reason, the digging ceased and the sobbing ramped back up. It lacked the pleading from before, and instead was laced with a sense of finality. Almost prayer like, similar to the sounds a person strung up at the gallows would make before the floor fell away.

The gunshot was deafening.

The second blast was muted by the shock that coursed through Tony's body. His breathing deepened, his head fell into his hands. Up until now it was all assumption; deep down he hoped for some kind of rational explanation, that it would all just be a humorous misunderstanding. The gunshot confirmed it. Equally worrisome was the fact that he really was on his own if there was no use for a silencer or knife. That or the locals turned a blind eye. Neither option offered any comfort.

One of the men said something that elicited a bout of laughter.

Then the burial began.

There were two shovels at work this time. The actions were quick and purposeful. In less than ten minutes it was complete. Boots stomped down on the replaced earth, compressing their work.

The car engine rumbled back into life.

The distant glow of the headlights was again visible through the canvas walls of the tent.

Tony held his breath, lips sucked in.

The vehicle let out a whine as it reversed.

The gate creaked closed.

All that was left was the jangle of the chain being replaced and the padlock snapping shut.

The car idled.

The rumble of the engine masked an exchange between the two men.

The sickness rose from Tony's gut and burned his throat. His eyes were screwed tight, his fists clenched tighter. He begged to hear the metallic sound of chains being collected from the ground.

Instead, there was the rustling of footsteps moving through long grass.

Tony's tensed arms were crossed around his chest; they shook to the rapid beat of his racing heart. "No. Please no," he whispered.

The footsteps neared, becoming louder and more defined with each step.

The walls of the tent closed in; with each shallow exhale the sleeping bag constricted him inch by inch.

A shadow of an approaching figure began to grow over the canvas wall. It became larger with each step and came to a stop next to the minuscule tent. A black silhouette loomed.

Somewhere in the distance Tony heard the beginnings of the dawn chorus. A tear streaked down his face.

The shadow squatted down. "Knock, knock."

Loblolly

The ship rocked to the rhythm of the gentle swell that lapped against its thick timber hull. Deep within the depths of HMS Arcade, far from any natural light and where the salty air was replaced with the scent of iron and alcohol, a frightened teenager waited. With black, shoulder length hair and smooth, youthful features, David stood in silence. From the several decks above, he'd heard an army of footsteps rush to their positions, but now it was replaced with a tense silence.

Two burly men stood to his side. Both dressed in grey, baggy shirts and thick cotton trousers, the men's harsh and severe faces were made all the more sinister by the flickering of the lanterns that hung throughout the cabin. Several weeks had passed since David was snatched from the streets by the roaming press gangs and dragged to the port, and even now he still didn't know their names. Instead, he mentally referred to them as Limp and Hunch, based on their physical imperfections.

There was one more person who resided within the damp and cramped confines of the infirmary. Beside the thick oak table, that was stained and scuffed from the multiple patients laid upon it, was Mr Slines, the ship's surgeon. With thick mutton-chops and dark cropped hair, the formal and intense man quietly cleaned his spectacles on the brown leather apron that was tied around him, unbothered by the events unfolding on the decks above.

Behind him, next to the steep stairs that led away from this dingy and damp cabin, were rows of shelves packed full of medical equipment and glass jars; some contained clear fluids, others were packed full of juicy leeches, and one was crammed to bursting with thousands of wriggling maggots. To the man's left side were pails of water scattered across the timber floor. To his right was a table upon which an arsenal of vicious-looking tools lay. A mere glance over the selection of knives, saws, hammers and pliers was enough to make David wince.

A shout came from somewhere high above. It sounded like the Admiral, his voice stiff and authoritative. The order caught the surgeon's attention. He placed the cleaned glasses back onto his face, resting them atop a thin, pointed nose, and moved his hands to grip the operating table.

David began to take deeper breaths. He could feel his heart pound against his chest, and his legs shake against the loose trousers that he wore.

Hunch made the sign of the cross in front of his chest.

Limp gripped one of the supports with a large hand.

There was a moment of stillness.

The hull let out a long creak, sounding as if it was resisting the pressure of a kraken's tentacles trying to squeeze the life from the flagship.

The thunder of thirty cannons exploding along the broadside made every bone in David's thin body shake. The force travelled through the ship like a shock wave, pulling the smoky odour of used gunpowder into the medical cabin with it. Frantic yells and orders immediately followed, barked from a commanding officer somewhere high above. Behind the nasal, formal voice, somewhere off in the distance, a faint booming noise could be heard. David didn't have time to place the sound before it was snuffed out by the shattering of wood and the screaming of men. The enemy had returned a volley of fire; the iron balls ripping through the ship's interior, leaving a trail of splinters, smoke and mutilation in their wake.

"Look sharp, Loblolly," Limp ordered.

David's new future was that of a Loblolly Boy, so named after the thick porridge served to sick and injured crew members. The new duties of his enforced career now included cleaning surgical instruments, disposing of body parts and obeying any other whim that Mr Slines or his assistants asked of him.

During the teenager's short time aboard the ship, he'd witnessed all manner of surgical procedures, if they could be called that. From the blood-letting that filled the leaky pails with pints of warm blood, to teeth removal via a set of tarnished iron pliers plunged deep into the gaping mouth of an unfortunate individual. With one leg pressed up against the patient's chair, and two hands wrapped tightly around the handle, Mr Slines would pull until his arms shook and his veins pulsed. The muffled screams of the poor man would be briefly silenced with a faint popping noise, followed by a tidal wave of blood that flowed from the man's whimpering mouth. The surgeon would hold the offending molar up to the dancing flame of the lantern and with a proud nod, turn and drop it into a glass jar with the others he'd collected.

The cannons detonated again, catching the teenager off guard and causing him to lose his balance. He stumbled into one of the assistants. The man didn't flinch; it was like David had knocked into a huge oak tree.

"God damn it, Loblolly," Hunch spat.

Before he had a chance to defend himself, the first casualty appeared at the entrance hatch. Sat with his feet dangling into the cabin, his injury was immediately evident. A 24-pound sphere of hardened metal had torn through the ship, taking the lower half of the man's right leg with it. The crewman was crazed, clawing at his shipmates and begging not to be lowered into the dark confines. Limp and Hunch grabbed the man by the waist and pulled him down the steep steps, laying him across the operating table. The man thrashed within the grip of the two henchmen like a fish caught in a net.

David looked on at the crewman's mangled stump, suppressing a rising sickness within him.

"Is it just your leg?" the surgeon asked, unfazed by the injury or distress before him.

With wide, panicked eyes, the injured man rapidly nodded his head.

Mr Slines collected several of the surgical instruments and dropped them into one of the nearby pails of water.

In his old life, David was a printing press operator and as a result was more educated than he liked to let on. He was literate from a young age, and of the many things he had read, one of them was William Beatty's accounts as a surgeon at the Battle of Trafalgar. Although the details of those memoirs did little to calm his nerves now, the Loblolly Boy was faintly aware of what surgery involved. He remembered that Admiral Nelson requested the surgical instruments to be warmed before a procedure as a small gesture towards the patient, which presumably explained Mr Slines' actions.

"David, bring over the tourniquets." The surgeon's voice was calm and measured.

The ship violently jerked to the side, accompanied by another outburst of agony from one of the other decks. A queue of disfigured and maimed patients would soon form.

David returned with the screwed contraptions. With Limp and Hunch holding the panting sailor down, David wrapped a sheet over the man's thigh. Sliding the tourniquets up his leg, he tightened the screws, so compressing the arteries and stemming the blood flow.

Nodding at David's handiwork, Mr Slines reached down and retrieved a long, curved knife from a pail next to him. Its stained blade reflected a dim glow from one of the nearby lanterns.

Just as the knife was about to be plunged into the man's leg David called out, struck by another memory of those historical accounts.

"Wait! Shouldn't we give him something to bite on?"

The two henchmen peered down at the boy and scoffed.

"We don't have anything," Mr Slines announced impassively. "There's no time." And with that he drove the blade forward, sinking it deep into the patient's calf. With one hand pulling on the skin below the incision, the surgeon made a slick move with the weapon, slicing through the muscle and tissue, causing it to come away like old, peeling paint.

With a desperate cry, the man kicked out, his body rising several inches from the table until it was overpowered and forced down by the strength of Limp and Hunch. The surgeon lent back and with the tip of his tongue poking out through his thin lips, admired the fresh, butchered flesh. His gaze dropped to the bloody knife he still wielded, then finally to the tortured face of the sailor.

David watched from a distance, aware that speed was imperative during an amputation; a requirement that didn't seem to concern Mr Slines. The unhurried surgeon glanced over.

"Is there a problem, Loblolly?" he asked over the wailing of the patient.

David shook his head, unable to take his eyes off the scene that was unfolding before him.

The surgeon gave the briefest of nods and tossed the blade onto the side table, and reached back into the bucket of water, retrieving a glistening tenon saw.

David had seen Mr Slines handle the saw once before when he'd walked in on him unannounced. The surgeon was banging the serrated edge against a set of chains. The high-pitched screech of metal on metal caused the teenager to flinch as he'd tried to get the man's attention. Upon seeing the Loblolly Boy standing there, Mr Slines had immediately stopped and thrown the saw to one side.

The cabin rocked again from another volley of cannon fire. The shattering of cladding and splinters echoed around the ship. The surgeon didn't react, however, his concentration focused on the crimson hands that wrapped around the wooden handle of the straight-edged saw.

Briefly licking his lips, the surgeon went to work. David was certain he saw the tiniest glint of a smile creep across the face of Mr Slines the moment the grinding sound of dull metal on bone filled the cabin. His action was slow and steady, with long, drawn-out cuts, as if ensuring a fine and plush finish. The screaming of the crewman was now unbearable, drowning out the cannon fire and battle that raged above.

David screwed up his eyes and pressed his hands against his ears, wanting to escape the horror. It had been several minutes now; the amputation should have finished long ago. The wailing and cries grew louder and louder, with David pressing harder and harder over his ears, failing to block out the screams, until, suddenly, there was silence.

Tentatively, David opened his eyes, afraid of the sight that awaited him. The crewman lay sprawled on the table, his chest rising and falling in the unconscious cadence of a man who'd just passed out.

The surgeon sighed and then with an increased, rapid motion, sawed through the remainder of the bone. The severed limb fell to the floor like a rotten branch.

"Well don't just stare at it, Loblolly," Hunch ordered.

David scurried forward and knelt at the feet of Mr Slines. The surgeon's eyes were wide. He sucked in deep lungfuls of stale air through a gasping mouth—a mouth whose corners were ever so slightly upturned.

With the warm, discarded limb in hand, he went to stand when another volley of cannon fire was released from above. He stumbled again, falling into the shelves and snatching at anything to keep his balance. A drawer was pulled open, spilling its contents onto the bloodstained floor. Looking down, David gasped at the sight of several unused bite pieces, every one of them devoid of indentations or teeth marks.

"Will you be careful?" Mr Slines cursed, now out of his joyful moment.

David shyly nodded and knelt down to collect the items. His mind was racing. Checking that the others weren't watching, he dipped his hand into the bucket containing the surgical instruments.

It was frigid.

He frowned and retracted his hand. He needed to check a final thing before telling the Admiral, just to make sure.

Hesitating for a second, he licked his wet fingers.

It was seawater.

With colour draining from his face at the realisation of what the surgeon was doing, he glanced up to see Mr Slines staring down at him with narrow, cold eyes.

"Do we have a problem, Loblolly?"

"No, not at all," David stuttered. "I just, just need to see the Admiral about something."

Before Mr Slines could reply, a rush of hot air and shrapnel engulfed the surgery.

A bright, white light blinded David. A high-pitched ringing filled his eardrums. He was aware of a burning sensation in his arm. For several moments he stumbled around disorientated until finally, his senses recovered.

He saw the surgeon and his henchmen straighten themselves from their cowered position, apparently only suffering a few minor wounds from the enemy's artillery.

The Admiral. I need to see the Admiral, David thought, his twisted reality now rushing back. The pain in his arm returned too. Holding it up into the air, he looked on in stunned silence at the bloody stump that now replaced his hand.

Flanked by his assistants, Mr Slines stepped forward with an evil grin across his face.

"Looks like we have our next patient."

Park Life

(First published in 'Black Dog, Black Tails' anthology, May 2020)

"You know, you shouldn't give them bread."

The unsolicited comment didn't cause Ernie to pause. One frail and arthritic hand held a mound of breadcrumbs, the other doled out the offerings to the circling ducks. Evening rays from the winter sun sneaked under a low-sitting flat cap, causing Ernie's wrinkled, jaundiced eyes to squint more than usual. He cocked his head and glared at the fellow park-goer, who'd joined him on the bench, so eager to express his opinions.

The man appeared to be in his early twenties. Clean-shaven – or maybe he'd not started yet – with a nonsense haircut that looked fresh from one of those stylist places. A dark suit jacket and open shirt struggled to contain a gut that was breaching over his denim waistline. The park was crawling with these types since the new call centre opened nearby, each of them annoying in their own unique way. It appeared that this upstart's special talent was doling out opinions to strangers. "Hasn't done them any harm for the past twenty-odd years."

"It causes all sorts of problems," the twenty-something persisted, validating Ernie's initial judgement. "There's no nutrients in the stuff, pollutes the water, and attracts pests. And the ducklings don't learn to forage properly."

"Is that right?" The plastic wrapper at Ernie's side rustled as a hand retrieved another scoop of breadcrumbs. From across the pond, swans glided silently toward the free meal.

"Yep, hold on two secs." Fingers tapped away at a smart phone screen; a succession of electronic bleeps provided another interruption to this otherwise pleasant spot. Ernie continued to watch the approaching swans. "Here we go. See?" The phone was thrust out, held between five podgy fingers.

"I'll bear it in mind." Another handful of feed was tossed out.

"You didn't even—doesn't matter." The phone was stuffed into a leather satchel. With some effort, the younger man pulled himself up off the park bench. A sticky name tag was stuck to his chest. "Alex" was scrawled in red pen under bold printed letters that read: Hi, my name is... Evidently, it was someone's first day. Alex was about to leave when a sudden thought rooted him to the spot. "You've been coming here twenty years?"

Ernie looked up with a raised eyebrow. "Twenty-four."

"Shit. That's older than me." A look of admiration spread across Alex's face. "Same bench?"

"Nope." Ernie brought his attention back to the ducks, deliberately pausing for effect. "Been replaced twice."

Alex let out a stifled laugh. "I guess coming out here keeps you young, yeah? Like, feeding the ducks and the fresh air and stuff."

"That's part of it." The last of the breadcrumbs were emptied onto the ground. Several of the less timid ducks left the safety of the water and waddled up between Ernie's scuffed brown shoes, picking at the scraps.

"Twenty-four years," Alex muttered to himself, as though struggling to grasp the enormity of the fact. With a raised voice, he asked, "Bet you seen some things?"

Ernie leaned back into the bench and watched the ducks squabble over the last of the food. "You could say that." If the truth were known, there were few events of notable exception Ernie had witnessed over the past quarter-century. A new playground was installed a few years ago. The gravel track around the perimeter was replaced with asphalt about a decade past. And there was the time when the pond was drained for some reason or another. He scanned the park, the glare from the sun now obscured by distant trees. The runners and dog walkers on the far side were reduced to animated silhouettes. Ernie brought his gaze up to meet Alex's. "It's the others, really, who give me a reason to return."

"Like, people watching?"

"If that's what your generation calls it. I'd say it was observing."

"Sounds a bit like stalking," Alex said. The accompanying burst of laughter was quickly muted when it became apparent he was the only one who found the joke humorous. "Sorry, I didn't mean to-"

Ernie waved off the faux pas.

Alex shuffled on the spot. "Is there anyone else who's been coming here as long as you?"

Ernie gestured with a small nod towards the other side of the pond. A skinny teenager skulked along, dressed all in black. A hood was pulled up and hands were dug deep into pockets. A black Labrador trotted along behind, a broad grin across its face in complete contrast to its owner.

Alex watched the pair for a moment, a frown deepening with each passing second. "That kid? But I thought you said you'd been coming here for twenty-four years?"

"I didn't say anything about the kid."

"The dog?"

Ernie let out a long exhalation. "Yep."

"That dog's been coming here all this time? Must be a different..."

"It's the same one."

"But they only live what, ten, fifteen years? Can't be."

"It is. It's the owners who change." Ernie adjusted himself on the bench.

"That bummed out teenager isn't the first?"

"Won't be the last either."

"Sorry?"

"That mangy thing has been ruining people's lives for decades."

"The Labrador? The one with the huge grin? How, by being too cute?" Alex said with a snort.

"You think that teenager always looked like that? I remember when he was younger. They used to play football over there, where those two trees are." Ernie pointed a knobbly finger towards a patch of flat grass with a pair of trees ideally positioned for goalposts. A group of boys were preparing for a kick-about. "Back then he was a star player. I used to watch him run circles around the other kids. When they picked sides, he was always the captain. Never arrived on his own; nor left for that matter. There was always a circle of friends around him."

Alex shrugged. "So, he discovered heavy metal and grew out of team sports. So what?"

Ernie looked Alex up and down. "I'm guessing you were one of the ones who was picked last?"

"No." The speed at which Alex defended himself suggested otherwise.

"Thought as much," Ernie said with a smirk, and brought his attention back to the sulky teenager. "Anyway, the day he turned up with that animal, it all changed. He got it to sit next to the goalposts while they played. The mutt never took its eyes off its owner the whole time. Watched him like a hawk. Anyway, the boy didn't score a single goal. The ball ended up in the water on more than one occasion; the poor kid had to go in and get it."

Alex gazed at the pond. "Meh, we all have bad days."

"A couple of months after that I noticed the boy was leaving alone. Well, apart from that dog for company. All the other kids would be in groups of twos and threes. He'd be at the back. Wasn't long until the games started without him and would end just as he turned up. The games he did make it in time for, he hardly seemed to touch the ball, even when he was put in goal. That occurred more and more too. All the while, that Labrador would stare up at him with those adorable eyes."

While Ernie had been speaking, the teenager had come to a stop. From the park bench, they watched as he looked over at the kick-about that had now commenced. The teenager lifted a hand to his face. The raised hood obscured the action, but not the slumping of his shoulders. The hand was forced back into a pocket and he continued, the Labrador in tow.

"You're telling me a dog did all that? No chance. The kid became a teenager. Probably got into weed and girls."

Ernie considered Alex out of the corner of his eye. He went to say something but held his tongue.

Alex checked his watch and looked out toward the reds and oranges of the sunset. "Anyway, I best get—"

"—Like I said, he's not the only one."

Alex hesitated. The time was rechecked. With a grunt, he dropped himself down onto the stained slats of the bench. "All right, go on, I'm listening."

A sly grin crept across Ernie's face that exposed two rows of yellowing, spindly teeth. "Well, the owners before that unfortunate kid were this young couple, lovely they were. At least, to begin with. They'd walk through here a few times a week, arm in arm and all that. You know, that kind of first love that—ah, you probably don't."

Alex flinched at the remark.

"Anyway," Ernie continued, "you should have seen them when they got that dog. Don't ask me how; it just seems to turn up like an unwanted guest." Ernie let the comment hang for a moment before continuing. "They doted on that mongrel as if it was their child. Playing on the grass. Throwing balls and sticks. Endlessly feeding it treats. It didn't last long, mind."

"They get bored with it?" Alex asked.

"Got bored of each other, I'd say. That loving embrace doesn't last forever. Least, not what I've seen. They may have walked arm in arm, but I could feel the tension from here. As I'm sure you know, looks can be deceiving."

Alex unsubtly sucked in his stomach while adjusting himself on the bench. "What do you mean by—?"

"—Soon they were holding hands. Not long after that, they walked side by side. The dog filled the ever-growing void between them. They'd stopped playing with it by that point. The grin never faded from its face, though. A month or two later, only the woman was out walking it. I remember it well, was an overcast day, the clouds thick with rain, and she was out with these over-elaborate sunglasses. Who did she think she was, Audrey Hepburn?"

Alex looked on bewildered.

"Look her up on your flashy phone later."

Alex shook his head and folded his arms. "So, you reckon the dog drove them apart?"

Ernie shrugged. "I'm just saying what I saw." He opened and closed his hands, then sat up straight and stretched out his back. The old joints satisfyingly popped and cracked. "It was the same thing with that jogger."

"The jogger?"

"You know, a runner. I guess someone of your stature would not be familiar with—"

"—I know what a jogger is," Alex snapped. His folded arms tightened around his chest, pushing out his stomach ever so slightly.

"Of course." With an ever-increasing smile and a voice growing louder and full of confidence, Ernie said, "Well, anyway, she used to go at a hell of a pace. With her sweatband and fancy shoes, I would often see her passing other runners. The dog would trot along behind, smiling away as he does, taking no interest in the other runners or cyclists.

"Over time, the woman's pace started to slow. She was never one to be overtaken, but there was the odd time. That grew to a few. Soon she was being lapped. The sweat would be pouring off her. The mixture of exhaustion and frustration never left her face and only got worse as more and more people passed by."

"She was probably injured or something. Or getting old." Alex gestured toward a chipped and scratched wooden walking stick that rested against the end of the bench. Ernie glanced at the walking aid, then shot Alex an unimpressed look. "Sorry." Alex held up his hands. "I didn't mean it like that."

"It wasn't either of those things, believe me. A few weeks later the woman had swapped running for walking, the faithful mutt always at her side. The confident strides became weary steps. Between you and me, she started filling out a bit, too.

You know those protein shakes the health nuts drink? Actually, you probably don't, but she used to be one of them. Knocking back the green smoothies at the end of each run. The last time I saw her, she was slouched on a bench just like this one, face buried in a bag of chips. It's amazing how people can let themselves go, don't you think?"

"I... I dunno." Alex was staring at the grass between his feet. The ducks and swans had long since left.

"Anyway." Ernie clapped his hands together and jumped to his feet. The movement startled Alex out of his stupor. "Alex, wasn't it? I best be going. Been a long day. Probably going to be even longer for you."

Alex slowly raised his gaze. The last of the evening's rays caused him to wince. He struggled to get the words out. "What, what do you—"

"Yep, you have a good evening now." With wide alert eyes, Ernie flashed a broad smile of ordered, glistening teeth.

Alex could only manage a shake of his head as he watched the once old man, now full of vigour, stride away down the footpath. Alex blinked several times, struggling to find the energy to do much more.

Everything felt heavy. Ernie's walking stick remained, the wood pitted and pockmarked. Alex intended to call out and remind him; he just needed to catch his breath first. As he did so, a familiar black Labrador trotted up to the bench. The black-clad teenage owner was nowhere in sight. Without a moment's hesitation, the Lab clasped the walking stick within its grinning jaws and chased after Ernie.

When Worlds Collide

I sprinted down the brightly lit corridor, my hands and shirt covered in Franklin's blood. "Shut the thing down!"

The whirring of the machines was deafening. I stumbled through the laboratory doors, startling Jacob in the process. He burst up from his chair, sending it wheeling across the room and into the console. He clambered around his desk, bumping into it in the process and scattering several piles of paper.

I frantically pointed at the control station located on the other side of the lab. Crimson droplets flew from the kill key I gripped in my hand. Less than a minute ago it was hanging around my colleague's neck. "Your key," I cried, not breaking my step.

Jacob skidded on the tiled floor, almost falling to his knees as he tried to change direction. If he questioned my instruction I didn't hear it. The machines were operating at full intensity, drowning out any chance of verbal communication. *Were they ever this loud?*

The coloured bulbs on the console blinked in an epileptic frenzy. A klaxon was sounding somewhere, its shrill adding to the chaotic cacophony.

Arriving at the control station, with a pounding heart and weak legs, I was confronted with an array of dials, buttons and switches. My hands searched the mass of electronics. My vision was blurred; the options before me started to merge and become hazy.

I slammed a fist onto the steel top. "God damn it, where is it?"

I looked across towards Jacob. He stood less than five metres away but my eyes struggled to adjust, the blinking of lights behind him becoming more and more distracting. Some were beginning to flash in unison. Jacob waved his arms, catching my attention. His usually round and cheery face was now pale and drawn. His key was already inserted, a hand poised in readiness.

I could see that a clear plastic cover was flipped up. I searched for it on the control station and finding it, I yanked the thing open and jammed in the kill key. I met Jacob's wide-eyed stare, and began counting to three with my fingers.

With a hand in the air, I extended my thumb and mouthed one.

I blinked, trying to focus on Jacob and not on the flashing patterns that were emerging behind him.

I extended a second finger and mouthed two.

Jacob nodded along. The shrill of the engines caused me to wince. They shouldn't be that loud. I squeezed my eyes tight, trying to cower from the flashing bulbs. But in their place was that horrendous mental image I had run from less than a minute before.

I forced my eyelids open and extended a third finger, but my concentration shattered before I could mouth the number. I shook my head in disbelief. Every light source in the laboratory strobed in unison, whether it was the bulbs lined up across the console, the halogen strip lights hanging from the ceiling or the tiny LEDs on the computer monitors.

Something hit me and bounced onto the floor. Snapped from my stupor, I saw a notepad land at my feet. Looking up, I could see Jacob flashing in and out of view. He was desperately trying to get my attention. Whatever he shouted at me was drowned out by the animalistic cries of the machines. He held his hand in the air with three fingers extended. With a nod of his head, we turned the keys in unison.

Everything went black...

Up until several minutes ago it had been just another typical day in the lab, if your lab happened to be the kind that experimented with smashing atomic particles together. It's similar to the work undertaken by the Large Hadron Collider, but on a far smaller scale. But that was not to belittle our research. We still had several kilometres of magnetic tunnels to get those particles up to speed, and the results were just as spectacular and intriguing, often raising more questions than answers.

The machine was Franklin's brainchild, and he guarded it like an overbearing father. A studious, wiry man, his life revolved around the lab. He was the first to arrive and last to leave, and was often seen wearing the same clothes for consecutive days. It's not uncommon to meet people such as Franklin in this line of work; passionate and brilliant, but also socially awkward. When asked how he was, the reply was always the same: "Busy." I'd never seen him laugh when a joke was cracked. He would smile, but I suspected that was because he knew it was polite to do so.

Jacob and I were contractors; hired guns brought in to assist with the operating of the equipment and attempt to derive any meaning from the results. It was straightforward work: fire up the machine, collide a few million sub-atomic particles, then wait for the data. After sufficient number crunching, the computer would produce spectacular illustrations. They were some of the most beautiful displays of quantum physics I'd seen in my thirty-year career; an entire spectrum of colourful lines that burst forth and ricocheted in all directions.

They wouldn't have looked out of place hanging in the Tate Modern. We awaited them with anticipation, and they made up for having to endure Franklin's company.

It was earlier today that Jacob and I started to notice that our colleague was acting strangely, even by his standards. It coincided with the graphic results failing to materialise. Jacob and I huddled around the matt black monitor, peering at our distorted reflections, waiting for results which never came.

However, Franklin was at his desk, his nose mere inches from the computer screen.

My eyes narrowed as I gazed upon him. "You got the results there or something?"

Franklin remained perfectly still. A pair of suspicious eyes spied me over the top of the monitor. "No."

My question was meant as a joke, but then again, it was Franklin. I tried again, this time a little more direct. "Shouldn't they be up on the screen by now?"

Franklin tapped on his keyboard. The image reflected in his glasses disappeared. "Probably broken."

Jacob and I looked at each other; this was a man who polished the bulbs on the console and knew every line of code in the programming. It wouldn't have been out of character for him to insist on us wiping our feet before entering the lab. There was no 'probably' in his world.

I shrugged it off and returned to my desk. I wasn't in the mood, knowing that I had mountains of numerical data to sift through.

At some point Franklin got up from his desk and hurried from the laboratory, returning some time later.

The day continued like this. With the machines being fired up, the experiment coming to an end, and Jacob and I gathered around the monitor while Franklin remained at his desk. Each time the graphics failed to be displayed was waved off with a variation of the 'must be broken' line. During the fourth or fifth experiment, once Franklin had left, Jacob came over to my desk.

He placed a hand on my computer monitor. "I see Franklin has left us again."

I rolled my eyes. "Seems a pattern's forming."

"You noticed he goes via the printer each time?"

I shook my head. I'd not been paying that much attention to the squirrelly man's movements; I had been focusing on analysing all this data. But now I was curious. I got up and wandered over to Franklin's desk and nonchalantly looked at his monitor. "He's locked it."

I glanced down and saw pages of scribbles. There were no letters, words or numbers but instead an array of mysterious symbols that repeated themselves across the paper. Some were circular, full of spirals and ovals; others were made entirely of straight lines that centred on a single point.

The doors to the laboratory whooshed open. "What are you doing?" Franklin demanded. He seemed tired, more so than usual. Dark bags had formed under his bloodshot eyes. He paced towards the computer, appearing to relax when he discovered that it was locked out.

I looked him up and down. "Everything all right?"

"Fine. Just... just an upset stomach." Franklin pulled his chair around and dropped himself down, avoiding eye contact in the process. He slid the notes into a drawer. "What were you doing at my desk?"

I held up my hands. "Just seeing if the results had come up."

"It's broken, I told you."

I glanced over at Jacob, then down at Franklin. "All right. Was just asking."

I could feel Franklin's stare bore into the back of my head while I walked back to my desk.

The afternoon continued like this, the only variant being the increased speed at which the machines were run at and the extended periods Franklin was gone for. Upon each return it seemed as though he had acquired a new wrinkle, or his hair was a shade greyer.

I looked over the parameters for the next experiment—it had not been run at such high energies before. "You sure about this?"

I was answered with an impatient wave of the hand.

The test commenced, but this time Franklin scurried from the lab before it was complete. I watched the instrumentation dials spin wildly. Several red lights blinked into life. "This isn't right," I called out to Jacob over the metallic groan of the machines as they battled against the will of their masters. "I'm going to get Franklin."

I left the laboratory and paced down the artificially lit corridors. There were only so many places he could be. His rarely used office was empty, as was the meeting room. It was then that I saw the door to the men's toilet was ajar.

I pushed it open. "You in here, Franklin? It's making one hell of a..."

I was cut short by the sight of slick red ooze emanating from under one of the toilet cubicles. My pulse quickened. I ignored the 'out of order' sign hung on the door and started banging my fist against it. The flimsy door rattled and shook from the pounding. "Franklin! You in there?"

My demands became increasingly aggressive. I could hear the distant roar of the machines. With no other options available, I dropped my shoulder and barged the door open. The sight that befell me turned my blood cold. There, slumped on the toilet was Franklin. His head lolled to one side, his lifeless eyes looking right through me. His arms hung uselessly, the sleeves rolled up and his wrists covered in large gashes. Blood drained from them at a steady rate. His shirt appeared to have been torn open, his chest crisscrossed with scratch marks.

I took a step back, retreating from the horror. It was then that I noticed the images displayed above him. At first it appeared as though the walls were randomly covered in the graphic results the computer generated. But the further I moved back, the more the images began to take form. Like some terrible Rorschach test, a creature began to reveal itself.

A set of horns burst from a grotesque gargoyle-like head. Rows of eyes ran in parallel down its face, with each beady pupil staring deep into the soul of whoever was foolish enough to look upon it. The mouth, shaped like an inverted triangle, was filled with rows of jagged teeth that all fought for space within the gaping snarl. Hundreds of thick tentacles spawned from below, spreading out in all directions.

A scream—no, it was more of a growl—boomed through the corridors. For a second it appeared as though it was being emitted from this being on the wall.

The machines!

The thought snapped me from my trance. I edged forward, filled with a mixture of disgust and urgency. Reaching out, I prised the kill key chain from around Franklin's neck. His head rolled forward as I did so. I flinched. Tearing my attention away from the dead scientist, my gaze once again fell upon the image. It was inches from me now. For a second, I thought I felt its hot breath on my clammy skin.

That distant growl again.

A violent shake rippled through my bones. I snatched the kill key chain and dashed from the cubicle, screaming for Jacob to shut down the machines...

Now waiting in the darkness, it was impossible to avoid the image of the creature. It appeared everywhere I looked, forcing itself upon me whether my eyes were open or closed.

The sound of heavy breathing filled the laboratory. My hand squeezed the kill key, the only means I had to steady the shaking.

Something moved in the blackness. Items were knocked over and sent crashing onto the floor.

Then a heavy weight hit the ground with a thud.

"Jacob?"

D.S. Vitrine

Rick looks up from the nautical charts spread before him, his stare fixed on the radio. The electrical device is positioned upon one of the many shelves that line the lavish cabin, sandwiched between thick nautical history books and two empty bottles of expensive whisky.

He waits, brow furrowed. The sound of the ocean swell lapping against a thirty-five foot, top-of-the-range fibreglass hull fills the void.

What should be a tranquil moment is shattered by another burst of static from the radio. The creases of his weathered face deepen and multiply. It is not the white noise that bothers him—it's a regular enough occurrence to hear snippets of communication from other boats in the area—but the distant cries and yells lost within the static, as though fighting against it, desperate to be heard.

The unsettling noise ends as abruptly as it began.

Rick stands and paces to the radio, his tanned face etched into a worried frown. Before he has a chance to collect up the receiver, the haunting static kicks in again. From the depths of the white noise the faintest of cries can be heard. "Hello? Hello? Please, can anyone hear me?"

Rick grabs the radio receiver and holds it to his mouth. When the cries cease he blurts out, "This is Second Wave receiving. What is your position? What is your emergency?"

He waits for a response, hands shaking with adrenaline.

The airwaves return to silence.

Rick tries again, his voice louder this time as though it'll somehow make a difference.

It does not.

He turns his attention to the steep ladder that leads to the deck above. Afternoon sunlight streams in from the opening. "Shelly! Can you come down here please?"

Rick stares at the radio, demanding a response. His pulse thumps behind his ears. "Shelly!"

The light in the cabin dims as he calls her name. His eyes narrow. There wasn't a cloud in the sky last time he checked. And where the hell is Shelly?

Forgetting the radio, Rick moves to the base of the ladder. Cast in shadow, he begins to climb the steps. The first thing he sees is Shelly. Her sunkissed, bikini-clad figure is sat on the deck, knees pulled up to her chest. She stares at something off the port side.

Rick goes to call her name but her headphones are still in. He takes another step. What he sees roots him to the spot. Floating a few metres away is a relic of a ship. It's similar in size to his yacht, but with far more sails, all of which are tattered and worn. Apart from blocking the rays of sunshine over Rick and Shelly, they are of little use for sailing. The wooden hull is black and rotten; the ropes dangling from the masts are frayed and worn. The crew are nowhere to be seen.

Rick slowly steps onto the deck, never taking his eyes off this new arrival. The ship's name is printed in faded lettering on the side of the hull. "Hello? Anyone aboard... D.S. Vitrine?" His voice slows as he speaks the peculiar name aloud.

The enquiry elicits no response.

Shelly's voice is almost a whisper. "Where'd it come from, Rick?"

"How should I know? Did you not see it float up alongside us?"

"I was lying here listening to music. Then the sun disappeared, I opened my eyes and... and there it was."

Rick waves off the explanation, there are more pressing matters at hand. With as much authority as possible, he shouts, "You mind giving us a bit of space? Bit close, wouldn't you say?"

His request goes unanswered.

Frustration turns to curiosity as this mysterious boat continues to bob aimlessly in the water. Well aware of the opportunities that an abandoned vessel such as this may offer, Rick takes matters into his own hands. He tosses inflatable fenders over the side and, using a hooked pole, leans out and snares one of the sodden ropes that run along the outskirts of the boat. Within minutes the vessels are tethered.

"You're going aboard?" Shelly asks as Rick prepares to leap across. "Why?"

"To see where the captain is." Rick almost loses his balance skidding on the deck slick with green mould. He composes himself and surveys the area—there is no sign of a crew, no possessions, nothing. It feels as though the boat has been adrift for decades, even centuries.

Rick spies a square hatch cut into the deck. He shuffles over. The darkness below is absolute. Pulling out his phone, he switches on the torch and shines a beam of light into the blackness. A set of rotten steps leads down into the abyss.

"Be careful!" Shelly calls out.

Rick nods, gets down onto all fours and sticks his head under. The torch lights up a bare cabin save for what appears to be a collection of bottles at the far end. Satisfied that no one is around, he descends the stairs.

The cabin below reveals itself one slow step at a time. The low ceiling appears to bow under its own weight. Rotting wooden planks line the cramped interior, their moisture glistening in the torch's beam. He's drawn to the collection of glass bottles. There are dozens of them of varying colour, shape and size that once upon a time contained some sort of alcohol. However, in contrast to the rest of the ship, they appear brand new, gleaming as though polished. He prises his curiosity away and rushes back up the steps. "Shelly, you need to see this!"

After several moments of hesitation and persuasion, Shelly is aboard and stood next to him in the gloomy confines, torch in hand. Her shoulders are tense, her face screwed up in disgust. "What is this?"

Rick doesn't reply. Undeterred by the damp and grime, he moves towards the selection of bottles. Warped lengths of knotted planks flex under each footstep. For a moment he wonders how this boat is even afloat, never mind seaworthy. Arriving at the display, his mouth falls open at the sight of model ships impossibly contained within each glass prison. It appears the entire history of seafaring vessels is on display: rudimentary canoes, World War II destroyers, rowboats, merchant ships. There is even a submarine. The detail of each model is exquisite—sails have dedicated lines that are pulled taut, ships' names are inscribed into the hulls. Some of the naval battleships even have rows of cannons that poke out of the galleys like little black eyes. It is this final detail that invites a closer look. Rick clutches the bottle and holds it up to the light. There is an imperfection in the glass; a parallel row of tiny pit marks line the inside. He holds up the bottle to eye level—the indentations align with the cannons aboard the ship.

Shelly remains at the base of the ladder, the light from her torch scanning the interior. "Everything okay?"

Rick's stare does not falter. "You should see these. They're incredible."

Shelly says something in reply but he does not hear.

The bottle is held closer, centimetres from his squinting eyes. "Sangria," he mutters, reading aloud the cursive printed on the side of the antique galleon. The name triggers a memory. He stares off into the distance. Sangria. Then it hits him. This is the ship that was discovered off the coast of Ireland, a survivor of the Spanish Armada. It was one of the few that escaped along the Irish coast in retreat. The Sangria ground itself in the shallow waters, despite clear weather and visible hazards. There was no evidence of the crew abandoning ship; no rowboats were spotted out in the water. It was assumed that they were on board. After several days of inaction and a growing interest on land, a handful of fishermen rowed out. They were not greeted with hostility, neither were they greeted with welcoming arms. They were not greeted at all. The ship was deserted. The crew's belongings remained, plated food decomposed in the mess, the rigging was set and the rudder went unmanned. All the souls on board had simply vanished. Later it transpired, upon reading the captain's diary and discovering a sizable stash of gold, that the crew had betrayed the armada and fled the battle scene, no doubt aware of the carnage their devious actions would unleash on their fellow mariners.

Rick places the bottle back with a slight shake of his head. Another model catches his eye, that of a super yacht, the type owned by Saudi princes and media moguls. He angles the bottle so he can read the name on the back: Classy Date. He suspected so; there are not many yachts that have two helipads. Back in the early two-thousands, it was picked up by the coast guard as it drifted around the Horn of Africa, the crew absent along with any signs of a struggle or SOS's sent. Once the empty vessel was towed into port and inspected, a converted space in the hull was found for undocumented minors to entertain guests.

A small shiver rattles down Rick's spine. He feels dirty merely holding the bottle and it is quickly replaced. A thought crosses his mind—*how is this decrepit ship, that seemingly appeared from nowhere, have such recent models in its collection?*

Shelly says something but is silenced with a curt, "In a minute, doll." The gears within Rick's head are turning, grinding together and piecing together a pattern. A pattern that becomes more defined with each model ship that is recognised.

He runs a finger along the shelves, hastily checking each one.

There's the Pioneering Spirit, a super tanker that was found adrift in the North Sea. The crew missing, along with a million barrels of crude oil that it should have been transporting.

Then there is the racing yacht Cat Fish. It was competing in the America's Cup last year and ground to a halt midway across the Pacific. It later came to light that the captain had bribed a number of the officials during the qualifying stages of the race.

Shelly's voice again, her tone concerned and worried. "Rick, have you read what's inscribed on the wall here?"

But Rick isn't listening. He glances at the final bottle on the shelf and breath escapes his lungs. The shape of the hull is instantly recognisable, as is the pattern on the sail. He already knows that the name inscribed on the rear of the boat will read Second Wave.

An icy pulse rushes through his body as the pieces click into place. He collects the bottle up in shaking hands, struggling to comprehend what he is looking at.

As he does so, Shelly reads aloud the inscription carved into the wall. Her voice echoes around the cabin.

When the deeds are done, and they've lost their way,
The Devil may claim what the sea casts away.

The last line is accompanied by a shatter of glass as the bottle slips through Rick's hands. "We need to leave!"

Before Shelly can protest Rick is at her side, his fingers digging into her arm as she is violently spun around. He ascends the ladder two steps at a time, yanking himself up by the rotten handrails, towards the square of blue sky above.

But as he bursts from the gloomy confines he finds himself back on his boat. Confusion freezes him in place. They are alone on the water, but something is different.

Shelly collides into him, knocking him forward. "What is it? What is the..."

The realisation that they are back on their boat stops her mid-sentence. They exchange a worried look. Neither of them speaks. At that instant Rick notices an absence of rocking from side to side. The ocean appears worryingly still as though made from resin. He stares down into the space that they had just escaped from and sees the familiar cabin of their boat. Tentatively, he lowers himself down. The charts are spread across the table; the radio is on the shelf next to the thick history books and empty bottles of whisky.

Shelly is near hysterics. "What's going on? What's happening?"

It sounds like white noise to Rick. All he is thinking about is how this boat, his pride and joy, was bought with the cash from the company's pension fund, right before he sold his stocks and fled to international waters and foreign fishing ports.

He lurches for the radio receiver, fumbling it within unsteady hands, and cries out, "Hello? Hello? Please, can anyone hear me?"

Blind Faith

"It was the postman who noticed it first, that all of the bottles were still out. Imagine how weird that must have been, a whole village with two bottles of milk on each doorstep."

Adam addresses me from the crumbling altar, appearing to enjoy the grandeur of the position. His straggly hair and baggy clothing ensure that he would never be mistaken for a man of the cloth.

I nod along while admiring the shattered remains of the stained-glass windows behind him.

Unprompted, Adam continues, "During the Cold War it was—the height of the Cuban Missile Crisis. People forget that it wasn't just America that was on edge. Even the inhabitants of quaint English villages had their worries." He gestures with his free hand; the other occupied with holding a weighty crowbar. "This was where they worshipped. Then one day, the postie came through and thought it was a bit quiet, and saw all the milk bottles out.

"He knocked on a few doors but there was no reply, and when the alarm was raised they discovered a load of cars parked outside this church, but the place was empty as it is now." Adam's voice bounces around the ageing structure. "Some people thought they were Commie spies and had fled back to the motherland. Others reckon it was some kind of mass suicide pact; the pastor was a bit out there... so they say."

Adam jumps down from the altar and lands on the stone floor. "Not much left for the taking now though."

Adam and I are new additions to the long list of visitors who have explored this place. The mystery of the missing congregation has weathered the test of time far better than their place of worship. The church or what is left of it, stands defiantly against the endless encroach of Mother Nature. Three sides of the steeple remain, but at a drunken tilt, with the missing side having collapsed through the roof, ripping open a gaping hole and leaving splintered rafters in its wake. I step over the shattered slate and look up through the unintended skylight at the grey sky above.

The masonry walls have fared better against the onset of time but are defenceless against a more contemporary attack. Neon graffiti and incomprehensible scrawls paint the structure, inside and out, undermining the religious significance it once held.

Adam strolls towards the remains of the organ at the rear of the church. A number of moss-covered keys are missing. The grand pipes that extend to the ceiling have either toppled over or are disintegrating where they stand. Adam taps the crowbar in the palm of his hand as he walks. The sight of it makes me nervous. He's always on the lookout for a 'souvenir', as he puts it. It's not the first time that I wish I knew other urban explorers, ones who had the same knowledge as Adam when it came to rooting out these places, but with better scruples.

With a camera around my neck, I wander through the rotten pews. The majority of them have either been flipped over or smashed down to their bare bones. I drop to one knee in an attempt to frame a suitably eerie shot of the altar, organ, and shattered windows, but my attention is drawn to the stone paver under my foot. It rocks a little when I apply weight to it. Upon closer inspection, I notice that it lacks the grey outline of grout that all the others share.

Adam approaches. "What you got there?"

"Just a loose stone or... something."

"Let's have a look."

Before I can protest, Adam plunges the end of the crowbar into one side of the paver.

I leap back, barely dodging the end of the metal implement. "Woah! Woah, what you doing?"

"Never know with these places," he replies, his voice strained as he attempts to lever out the stone.

To my surprise, it begins to move, and with a little more encouragement, it starts to work itself free. A few more grunts and it's prised out and slid to the side. A cloud of dust takes its place. Before the particles have even begun to settle, Adam has a head torch strapped to his forehead and is staring at a set of concrete steps, descending into the murky darkness. "You coming?"

I point at the hole. "In there?"

"Yeah."

"But we don't know what's down there."

A smile creeps over Adam's face. There is a sinister glint in his eye. "Exactly."

I watch his silhouette move deeper and deeper into the void. The light from the head torch slicing through the darkness resembles a lonely lighthouse shrouded in mist. He suddenly freezes, transfixed on something out of my line of sight. "Jesus Christ."

My grip around the camera tightens. "What? What is it?" I pause and realise where we are. "Wait, you taking the piss?"

"Nah, mate. I think we found our congregation." Any playfulness in his voice is long gone.

My guard remains, however. It wouldn't be the first time that he's wound me up. Several months ago, when we were snooping around an abandoned hospital, Adam hid in a cupboard for over twenty minutes. While sniggering to himself, he listened to me calling out his name and becoming increasingly anxious; eventually he burst out, scaring seven shades of shit out of me.

With this in the back of my mind, I cautiously descend the stairs. Stale air fills my nostrils. With each step, I can feel myself sinking into the dank murkiness of the tunnel. I come level with Adam and shine my torch down the passage. The concentrated white beam lights up strings of rags that hang from the ceiling. There are more piled below, with what appears to be thin grey sticks mixed up within them.

"What am I looking...?" I'm stunned into silence as the torch beam illuminates a suspended spinal column that snakes its way up to a lopsided skull. It hangs there like some heinous decoration. It hits me that those rags are holding together skeletons, and the grey sticks that litter the floor are bones.

"The fuck is this place?" I have to force the words out.

Adam begins walking towards the grim discoveries. "Quite a find, I'd say."

"Where are you going?" I hiss, as if in danger of waking the dead.

"Mate, whatever happened here was a long time ago. No harm in taking a closer look."

I recognise that tone, and I can sense the smile on his face. It goes hand in hand with the crowbar at his side. I watch him as he squats down and begins going through the piles.

I rush towards him. "What the fuck are you doing?"

Unconcerned with my outburst, he looks up at me and brandishes a tarnished gold watch. He shakes it a few times and holds it next to his ear. His white teeth dazzle in the torchlight, and he returns to rummaging through the discarded remains.

I check over my shoulder out of fear that someone may have spotted us. "What is wrong with you? Have some respect."

"Don't be so melodramatic." He holds up a small bone and angles it upright, allowing the engagement ring to fall into his palm. "They 'ain't going to miss them."

I shake my head and try to avoid the swaying spinal columns that Adam has disturbed. It is then that I notice a symbol crudely drawn on the wall. I shine the torch around the passage and realise it's everywhere. It looks like a hammer and sickle, the kind found on the Soviet flag. But these are drawn within a circle, and with a line slashed through them. "Have you seen these?"

Adam doesn't miss a beat with his scavenging. "What? No."

Of course he hasn't. There are more pressing matters at hand. I watch him for a few moments, and once he is done, he stands and glances at the walls. "I dunno," he says with a shrug and continues down the tunnel. "You coming?"

I follow a few steps behind, not sharing the same enthusiasm. "We need to tell someone about this. About them." I gesture over my shoulder. I shudder at the realisation that we will have to pass the lynched victims on our way out.

"We will," Adam replies. "Let's just see what we're dealing with first."

The gloomy passage continues for tens of metres. Somewhere in the distance, I can hear the plop of water. Disturbed rats scurry past.

Up ahead, the torch beams illuminate a heavy wooden door. That same symbol—long faded but still retaining a red tint—is scrawled across the vertical timber slats. I notice scratch marks in it, as well as dents and chips.

There are more rags stacked up at the base of the door, as though someone left piles of filthy laundry to be dealt with later. With each step, they take on familiar and sinister shapes. Skeletal figures emerge from the darkness. Some are jumbled up against the walls; others lie stretched out, reaching towards the door. It dawns on me that we're in the depths of a mass grave. A sickness begins to brew within my gut. The air tastes sour; my eyes become sore and itchy.

"What do you think is through there?" Adam asks, barely slowing his pace as he approaches the entranceway.

I don't reply. My mind is preoccupied with what we have unearthed. I come to a stop and place a shaking hand on the wall to steady myself. I focus on my splayed fingers and realise that I have inadvertently placed my hand in the centre of one of the symbols. I can't seem to escape them. I look down to see a grey skull staring back at me, the jaw hanging open and the empty eye sockets darker than night.

I suppress the need to vomit and instead focus on the thick timber door. It is not unlike something that would have featured at the entrance to the church. But the destructive effects of time have reduced the once opposing force to something weak and beaten.

Adam doesn't use the crowbar. He doesn't need to. A few shoulder barges and something unseen on the other side, shatters. Another shunt and the door opens a few centimetres. I can hear furniture shifting and tumbling to the ground. Adam throws his weight at the door again, and it finally relents enough for him to squeeze through. He flashes another grin at me and disappears out of sight.

The thought of being left alone down here causes my pulse to quicken. I chase after him, and wriggle my way between the door and the frame. The timber presses against my clammy skin, and for a moment, I feel as though I'm going to become stuck; forever destined to be trapped down here in this place of death.

Squirming through into the simple, bare room, I see it filled with white light and stretched shadows. My attention is first drawn to the makeshift crucifix, which stands crooked in the centre. It appears to be constructed from a jumble of furniture. The sight of it reminds me of the derelict steeple above us. A heap of bones, wrapped in a cloak, lies at its base. A black and white clerical collar is visible under the skull and acts as a type of mount. As I draw the torchlight further from the pastor's remains, I see more, ever more bones and tattered clothing that fan out from the crucifix. They are smaller than those we've seen so far. Toys and playthings litter the ground.

My attempts at understanding what happened here, to try and piece together all the elements and make sense of this place, are interrupted by rustling and cursing. Adam is scavenging through the remains again. He throws his hands up in frustration and tosses a rattle to the ground. It lands on a teddy bear, causing a puff of dust to waft into the air. I watch the particles dance upwards in the torchlight, and the sight of the crucifix comes back into view. Everything clicks into place. My chest tightens. I kneel down and pick up a tattered buckle shoe that fits in the palm of my hand. A tear breaks free and streaks down my cheek.

Adam's voice echoes around the room. "Ah, this is a waste of time. There's nothing of value in here."

"There was," I mutter.

Time & Punishment

The double locks disengaged and the heavy door juddered open. Father Bannon stood in the entranceway. It was not possible to tell whether he was wincing from the racket or that he always had that look to him. His thin wiry frame appeared as though he could have slipped through the bars that encased the cell. He hunched over ever so slightly, like the beginnings of a wilting flower. Hands were crossed at his waist, a leather-bound book in his grasp. He cleared his throat. "May I come in?"

Ali chuckled to himself, exposing two rows of yellowed, disorderly teeth. "May as well, seeing as they've already opened up for you."

The priest offered a slight nod of thanks and stepped into the concrete-lined, five-by-five cell. "How are you doing, my child?"

"You can knock that shit off for a start," Ali said from his seated position on the thin mattress. An elbow rested on each knee, fingers were clasped together with his chin resting on both thumbs. Muscular arms were flexed, distorting the many tattoos that adorned them. "I'm happy to talk. It ain't gonna do no harm. But I ain't part of your flock. You're gonna leave disappointed if you were after a last-minute conversion."

Father Bannon straightened his back. "Of course. Of course." He spoke softly, almost apologetically. "Is there anything you would like to talk about?"

Ali tilted his head to face the visitor, breaking his gaze from the chipped and scratched wall that he'd been staring down for the past few hours. "You mean like repent or something?"

"No, no, I didn't mean it like that. It's just, well, sometimes individuals in your position like to talk. Perhaps reminisce about better times, or take the opportunity to get things off their chest."

The hairs on Ali's arms bristled. His scarred hands subconsciously opened and closed; sometimes he could feel the guard's crushed windpipe within his palms like a phantom limb. "I don't need no holy man dying for my sins. I know why I'm here."

"We can sit in silence if you prefer?" Father Bannon said. The offer hung in the air. "Or I can go if I'm not wanted."

"No, no. Sit yourself down." Ali tapped the bed next to him. He guessed that it wouldn't hurt to have a bit of company in these final moments.

The priest hesitated, remaining just inside the entranceway.

"You don't need to worry about me, Father. I may not agree with your life choices, but I ain't got nuttin' against you."

Appearing satisfied with this reassurance, the priest shuffled forward and perched on the edge of the bed.

Ali returned his attention to the same patch of wall that had held his interest for so long. If he was dragged from this cell and asked to recreate the one metre square on paper, he could duplicate every mark, scuff and etched-in lettering down to the individual scratch. "You know what's been on my mind, though?"

"Go on."

"Well, seeing as you asked." Ali grinned as he spoke. "The choices we make in life, you know? I read a quote once, on a poster or some shit, that said, 'You're exactly where you're meant to be'." Ali shifted on the uncomfortable bed and faced the priest. "You believe that?"

Father Bannon's expression remained blank, evidently unsure whether the question required an answer or not.

Ali replied for him. "I suppose you fellas think it's all part of the Big Man's great plan." He raised up his hands, fingers spread, and pulled them apart in mocking wonder.

Father Bannon let out a small laugh. "Something like that."

The first show of genuine emotion from the visitor spurred Ali on. "So tell me this, if you could go back and change anything, would you?"

The priest shrugged. "But what difference does it make, we can't."

"Come on, G." Ali slapped his legs, his eyes were mischievous. "I ain't got long. Play the game."

The visitor relented, his smile widening. "All right, if I had the chance, then no, I would not change anything. As you astutely pointed out, this is God's will, and I abide by it." The leather-bound cover of the thick tome carried by the priest was tapped as he spoke.

Ali nodded in agreement, deep in thought.

The priest leaned forward. "But what about you? If you had another chance, what would you do?"

"That's all I've been thinking on." Ali's voice drifted away. He pointed a finger into the air and outlined a small circle. "All this place is good for." He sucked in a long breath that inflated his broad shoulders. In that brief moment he appeared twice the size of the priest. He continued, confidence returning to his words. "I reckon I got three: joining T-15, robbing the store and that thing with the guard."

Ali stood and took the three paces required to arrive at the vertical bars that kept him captive. "You know the weirdest thing about those events, Father? The reason why they stick in my mind?"

The priest shook his head. Although he remained seated they were almost side by side within the enclosure.

Ali continued. "Each time I had the strangest case of deja vu." He turned and looked down at the visitor. "What does your book say about that? A glitch in the matrix or something."

Father Bannon shrugged. "I don't think there is an answer to that."

"You ever experienced it?"

"Once, yes," the priest replied, appearing thoughtful as a distant memory materialised. "Just before I joined the church as it happens. It is an odd experience, I'll give you that."

"You didn't take it as a sign for something?"

"A sign for what?"

Ali sighed. "I dunno." He ran a hand along the metal bars. They were cold to the touch. If it wasn't these bars there would have been others.

The door at the end of the corridor swung open. The sound of multiple footsteps and jangling chains announced that the meeting was over.

Ali squeezed the bars then stepped back into the centre of the room. His shoulders were back, arms at his side, hands rolled up into fists. His gaze was locked on the entranceway. "Looks like our time is up."

Father Bannon got to his feet and straightened out his dark suit. "I hope this was of some solace."

Ali's stance did not falter. "I guess we'll see, won't we."

Several guards stepped into view; the smug expression they all shared was unanimous.

Father Bannon stood between the standoff. His gaze dropped to the batons that each guard wielded. With a disapproving shake of his head, he shuffled past and out of view.

Ali remained, staring down the guards, his expression that of a weary warrior going into battle.

They listened in unison as the priest's slow and deliberate footfalls wandered the length of the corridor. Each step rang out like the ticking of a clock. The door slamming shut may as well have been the strike of midnight.

Ali noticed several of the guards tighten their grip around the weapons. He suspected that he would receive a send-off from the screws, a parting gift before he was marched to the chamber.

They piled into the cell, batons raised and unafraid to use them. Ali suspected his fist may have connected with one of the assailants but he couldn't be sure. Within seconds the barrage of strikes reduced him to his hands and knees. Several ribs shattered. Blood was already starting to pool. A well-placed steel toecap to his eye socket knocked him flat. His world slipped into darkness.

**

Ali had no idea how long he was out for. The agony that consumed his body made him wish that he had never woken up. He'd always planned to take his final steps with dignity, his head held high and owning the consequences of his actions, no matter how reprehensible they were. However, he did not imagine that the last few moments of his existence would involve being carried along by four blood-splattered guards. He was unable to open his mouth. Viscous blood swished around within, coating his tongue and lining his throat. Occasionally something small, hard and jagged would creep to the back of his gullet and he would be forced to swallow it down. His feet dragged along the floor behind him, deemed useless now that both legs were broken, fractured bones jutting out at horrid angles. It hurt to breathe, it hurt to think, it hurt to exist.

The miserable world into which he'd awoken was viewed through the narrow slit of the one eye that still worked. The lighting above was harsh. The high-pitched ringing in his head shouted down all other noises around him. A rough shape of an overweight man appeared, the blurred features gradually forming themselves into the image of the warden. The guards stopped a metre or two before their superior. The warden checked his watch. Something was said but the words were inaudible over the incessant ringing within Ali's skull. The heavyset man considered the prisoner for a moment, inhaled a deep breath, then pulled open the door, gesturing for the guards to continue.

A hospital bed awaited them. It was located in the centre of the chamber. A table next to the gurney was filled with glass items that Ali would not have recognised even if his vision had been twenty / twenty. The lighting was brighter in here, almost blinding. A faint smell of bleach hung in the air.

On a count of three, Ali was hauled up and unceremoniously dumped onto his death bed. A violent shock exploded through his broken body as he landed onto the crisp white sheets. He lay where he fell, unable to protest at the rough hands that worked at the restraints that seemed a little unnecessary considering the circumstances.

One of the guards moved in close to Ali's face. A bruise was forming under his left eye. Ali tried to smile at the thought that at least he'd landed one punch, yet the state of his jaw forced the expression into a grimace.

The guard said something. Ali couldn't hear it, but he did feel the caffeine-ridden breath on his face. Something wet landed in his eye, forcing it closed. He would be destined to enter the other side blind, bound and beaten.

The door closed with a muted thud. More words were spoken, but they were distant and muffled, as though spoken from the far end of a lengthy tunnel.

The scratch at Ali's forearm barely registered among the various barbs of pain that shouted for attention.

He lingered in the black agony for a few moments longer. The conversation with Father Bannon replayed in his mind. It kept the suffering from becoming all-consuming. If he only had another chance.

It was his last thought before the trauma subsided and he descended into darkness once again.

**

There was no pain. In fact, there was no... nothing. He was weightless, floating in the ether. Despite his eyes being closed he could make out light and shapes. Voices faded in. Recognisable voices. A dog barked somewhere. Opening his eyes he found himself standing in a backyard. He looked on dumbfounded at the strip of overgrown grass filled with tattered deck chairs, discarded bottles and empty pizza boxes. A waist-high chain link fence lined the perimeter, separating this sorry excuse of a garden from the many around it. Countless nights had been spent smoking, drinking and gambling away the hours in the official HQ of T-15. But the scene that Ali had been dropped into was memorable as it was the first time he'd ever visited. Many of the gang members—that would soon be referred to as blood—gathered around a fire pit despite the warm evening. On this night, however, they were strangers when a young and scrawny recruit arrived.

From his invisible vantage point Ali watched as an all-too-familiar kid wandered into the yard. Fake bravado oozed from this sixteen-year-old dressed in a stained sleeveless t-shirt and baggy denim jeans.

Ali knew what was about to happen.

The gang turned to face the teenager. The remains of a joint were flicked over the fence, then they charged, just as the guards had done minutes before the lethal cocktail was injected. At the time, Ali thought he'd stood his ground well and taken the initiation like a man. But witnessing it now as an observer, it was pathetic. The teenager was bent over, arms around his head in a futile attempt to defend himself against the rain of fists.

Unlike the assault in the cell, it did not last long and the dumb kid was only reduced to a single knee. The posture seemed fitting considering the occasion.

The attackers backed away, pleased with the show. While one of the men sparked up a new joint and handed it to the teenager with an accompanying pat on the shoulder, another withdrew a metal poker from the fire pit. A bucket was upturned and placed on the grass.

The new recruit's eyes widened. The end of the joint glowed red as a long inhalation was taken; then the teenager dropped to his knees and extended a hand. Ali winced as the branding-iron was plunged into innocent flesh. The recipient's expression remained steadfast. However, his shaking body betrayed the stoic stance. The smouldering metal was removed, a trail of smoke snaked into the air, and the gathered mass let out a cheer. The newest member of T-15 let out a stifled cry through gritted teeth. An opened bottle of tequila was handed to him that was emptied in several greedy gulps. It invoked a round of laughter and further cheering.

Watching from the sidelines, Ali ran a palm across the rippled scar on the back of his hand. The pain he experienced that evening never dulled with time. It was not just his body that was branded that night.

The glow from the fire pit grew brighter and brighter. A white light soon flooded the garden. The last thing Ali saw was the teenager hugging the man who scarred him. Then the intense light wiped the scene from view.

**

The white faded away to reveal a gaunt face, inches from his. Ali knew who it was, but struggled to accept it. Bleeding sores were scattered across pale skin. Cheekbones were angular and pronounced, and deep heavy bags underscored both eyes. A hood was pulled up to hide thinning hair. They met each other's gaze, and Ali could see that the person inside had died long ago.

A collection of bells rang out in the distance. This was evidently the signal that the reflection was waiting for. He licked cracked lips, nodded to himself, and turned and strode away from the unbeknownst standoff. Rows of cereal boxes and tinned goods lined either side of the departing figure. It dawned on Ali that they were in the convenience store, and he was about to bear witness to the moment that got him incarcerated. He remembered it now. He had to mill around at the back of the store, strung-out, waiting for the chatty cashier to finish serving some old woman. They seemed to talk for hours about the weather and the price of cigarettes and every other inane subject possible. His patience was already stretched to the limit. If they spoke any longer he would have stormed over and pistol-whipped the both of them. Thankfully the disturbed bells indicated that the woman had finally left. He needed to move fast before another talkative customer entered. Little did he know that fate had prepared something far worse.

Witnessing the final moments before the handgun was withdrawn, Ali cried out for the junkie to stop. There was the briefest of pauses in the addict's stride, as though a fleeting thought had passed through his cloudy mind. But it was too late.

Ali didn't need to see what happened next. He knew how it played out. He screwed up his eyes, but he could not escape the audible accompaniment of the robbery.

The screamed orders comprised slurred words and stumbled sentences.

A shaky panicked response.

The till shunting open.

Fists full of notes and loose change being stuffed into pockets.

Then the stern, authoritative voices arrived. The blue and red flashing lights were noticeable even through closed eyes.

The clicking of cuffs closing around a pair of skinny wrists.

The strobing lights flickered faster and faster, grew brighter and brighter. Ali was whisked away yet again, but this time wearing the smallest of grins. It was just his luck that two officers happened to arrive as he was holding up the store. If only the conversation between the clerk and the old woman had lasted thirty seconds longer.

**

He was all too familiar with the prison cell. He'd spent almost six months in that cramped place until he was transferred to death row. A double bunk bed was placed along one side. A toilet bowl and sink were in the corner. Pictures of women in various stages of undress were plastered across the masonry walls. Ali drifted at the end of the cell, under the barred window. Rays of evening light poured in but his form did not cast a shadow. At any moment his previous self would appear in the entranceway, escorted by a guard. In a few seconds a distant prisoner would cry out like an attacking Cherokee. It was the signal for the riot to commence and would be the last sound the guard ever heard. He would be thrown to the ground, his head colliding with the rim of the toilet bowl. While he withered in a bewildered daze, a coward would wrap their scarred hands around his throat.

Two sets of footsteps approached. As predicted, Ali came face-to-face yet again with a memory of himself. It was a vast improvement from the convenience store. He'd been clean since the sentencing and had benefitted from the prison gym.

The young guard that accompanied the prisoner appeared as though it was his first day on the job, having recently transferred from some administrative position. A pair of wire-rimmed glasses perched at the end of his nose, his dark hair was combed into a tight side-parting that glimmered in the light. "Okay, let's go." The order was weak and unconvincing. The end of a baton was jabbed into the lower back of the prisoner, encouraging him forward.

Ali saw a crooked smile grow across the prisoner's face. There was a matter of seconds remaining. His arms were flung out in an attempt to draw attention away from the guard. He screamed out for his double to stop.

The prisoner frowned. His head tilted to the side and the smile melted away.

The signal for the riot to begin was yelled out.

It was ignored by the preoccupied prisoner while he remained transfixed on something unseen at the end of the cell. Then reality snatched him back to the present. He blinked, shook his head and spun on the spot, his intent clear. But the hesitation had allowed the guard to slip from reach as he dashed away to deal with the rising chaos.

The prisoner moved to the cell entrance and peered out. Shouts and screams filled the hall as orange-clad inmates spilt out and swarmed the security booth.

"Please, don't," Ali yelled out over the din.

His double remained in place. A hand was run up and down one of the many iron bars that caged him. With a shrug, he turned and moved to the bunk bed. With arms crossed behind his head, he lay and closed his eyes as the riot unfolded around him.

**

The clattering of the cell door startled Ali from his slumber. His eyes shot open. The stained mattress of the upper bunk, and the rows of rusted springs that supported it, came into focus. He recognised it instantly. He'd spent almost six months staring up at it before... before he was moved to death row. But that meant...

Jerked into action, he swung his legs off the side of the bed. His feet landed on the concrete floor. He never would have thought the feeling of rough stone would be a reason to smile. He stood and paced the cell, the smile increasing with each step. He came to a stop under the barred window in the exact spot where he'd managed to give himself a second chance. It felt like a lifetime ago.

His hands were inspected in front of his face. The initiation scar remained, as did the numerous tattoos that crowded his knuckles and forearms. Beyond his hands he noticed a shadow cast across the hard ground. "God damn!" The outburst was accompanied by a clap. His hands squeezed together in joy.

The celebration was interrupted by a guard stepping into view. Just like the mattress, bedsprings and prison cell, Ali recognised him immediately. Those wire glasses and shiny side-parting belonged to a man who was once destined to fall under Ali's hand.

"I see you're up," the guard said, oblivious to how things could have played out in another life. "Excited to meet your new cellmate?"

Ali frowned. "Cellmate?"

"Sure you two will get on well." The guard leant into the cell, his voice lowered. "A word to the wise, may want to avoid the subject of children. It's got the fella into all sorts of trouble." He snorted at his own humour and pulled back into the entranceway. The new prisoner shuffled into view. The guard patronisingly slapped the new arrival on the shoulder while he spoke in a raised voice. "Isn't that right, Father?"

The prisoner winced and lifted his head to meet his new cellmate.

Ali's mouth fell open. "Father Bannon?"

The Snowman

From the upstairs window, I stare down at the white figure that waits in the back garden. A pair of unblinking eyes stare right back. The smug dotted grin never falters. The circular head is smooth and round, the body is perfectly proportioned. Even the arms seem to bend at the elbow and split into five smaller appendages at the end. What are the chances of finding two identical branches like that?

Then there is the clothing. The red scarf matches the band around the black top hat. It's like they have been retrieved from a Dickens novel. It all seems a bit too perfect.

The patter of light feet breaks the standoff. I turn to see the young architect emerge at the top of the stairs; dressed in pink pyjamas, her blonde ponytail bobs from side to side as she charges into her bedroom. "Are you going to read a story, Daddy?"

"Yep, be there now." I glance back at my adversary, arms crossed tight against my chest.

Did he just...?

My nose is almost pressed up against the window. I'm sure he was further from the house. The darkening skies make it difficult to be sure.

"Daddy."

"Coming, Sally." My breath fogs up the window, momentarily hiding the unwanted guest from view. I wait for it to clear, my gaze never falters. I want to be sure.

With a narrowing of my eyes, I pry myself from the vantage point and head into Sally's room, resisting the urge to quickly check over my shoulder in the process.

She is already tucked in, illuminated by the glow from the single lamp next to the bed.

"What would we like to—"

"'Twas the Night before Christmas."

Her enthusiasm causes me to smile. It reminds me of the nights my grandmother used to read the same story to me and my brother. Collecting the tattered book from the shelf, I perch on the edge of the bed. The first page is entirely taken up by an image of a living room from the Victorian era. I've seen it a thousand times. A Christmas tree, draped in decorations, stands proud in the corner. Stockings hang above the fireplace. A glass of sherry and mince pie have been left on a side table. The colours of the illustration are warm and inviting.

I begin reading. "'Twas the night before Christmas, and all through the house, not a creature was stirring, not even a mouse..."

I pause while my attention is drawn to the window in the illustration. A silvery moon shines bright, and on the snow-covered ground below is an oddly familiar white figure. *How had I never noticed that before?*

I try to continue but my voice is empty, my mind distracted. Something isn't right. "The stockings were... the stockings..." The book is lowered to my lap. "Sally."

"Yes, Daddy."

"Where did you get the hat and scarf for the snowman outside?"

"What snowman?"

The Life and Crimes of Danny Wilson

The bookshop was Danny Wilson's favourite. Everything was old. All of the contents were tired and dog-eared, their second-hand status surpassed long ago. The bindings were peeling and the pages yellowing, with many of the items being better suited to a museum.

The chipped and scuffed wooden shelves—bleached by decades of sunshine that poured in from the store's large bay windows—struggled to hold the millions of words that rested atop them. At some point in time the shelves had reached their stuffing capacity and as a result, weaving columns of books grew upwards from the carpeted floor. Some were chest height, and Danny could never work out what the procedure was for obtaining a desired book if it was in the lower half of the stack.

The jingle of the bell that hung above the entrance door signalled the start of his day. The quiet, peaceful retreat was a world away from the chaos and darkness of his past life. For up until several years ago, Danny was a hired hand, employed by the more unsavoury characters around town that required his... persuasive qualities. But now, those days of violence existed only as unsettling memories that stalked Danny from his one-bedroom apartment, through busy streets full of strangers, to the front door of his haven. Once that bell rang he was free, absorbed by a world of words that transported him away from his afflictions.

Most days were spent with Danny sat in one of the two leather chairs provided for customers, reading through an endless supply of books, with only the gradual movement of the shadows that the window-panes cast, indicating that time was passing.

Today began no different from any other. Danny woke from the screams of his past victims—their cries silenced until it was time for another restless night's sleep. He ate porridge made with cold water and dressed his weary, hulking frame into one of the many identical charcoal suits that hung within the wardrobe. Lunch was prepared—a sliver of ham between two buttered slices of white bread and a piece of fruit—and he set out on the thirteen minute and twenty-four-second commute. Passing unfamiliar faces on the street, that were adorned with familiar, untrustworthy expressions, he marched towards his place of solitude.

The bell chimed as Danny stepped into his sanctuary, leaving the chaos of his past life waiting for him outside. He offered a respectful nod to the owners—an elderly couple who showed little interest in his daily visits. It had crossed his mind as to whether they minded him being here. He used to buy the books and read them at home, but as the time he spent on that leather chair lengthened, and his murky past became more certain, he found that the days in the store grew longer and longer. Often he would spend them undisturbed, with the bell above the door only sounding when it was time for him to leave. His only interruptions would be the need for sustenance, whether that was food or knowledge in the form of lunch or a new story.

And it was on this day, no different from the hundreds of others that came before it, that he discovered a book that would change his life forever. Running a finger along the crowded shelves, he browsed the library for a new means of escapism and came to an abrupt stop at a particular offering.

The first detail that caught his attention was the condition of it. Wedged in alongside the usual tired, time-ravaged tomes, this book looked like it was still in the packet. The spine was perfect, not a crease on it, and the royal blue colouring and gold lettering were vibrant and vivid, as if still drying, fresh off the printing press.

The second and more intriguing detail was the title, written in an ostentatious, overly-elaborate font. He lightly mouthed the words as he read it: "The Life and Crimes of Danny Wilson."

He blinked several times then withdrew the biography, revealing a final detail that froze Danny in place. Printed on the cover, in black and white, was a close-up photo of someone who bore the same rough and worn features as he did. A balding scalp, crisscrossed with thin, trailing scars, crowned a misshapen face that appeared to have been remoulded from years of brawls and punch-ups. A stumpy fat nose sat in the centre of the man's imposing sneer and deep-set, harsh eyes added to the hostility of the expression. The photo reminded Danny of the life he was keen to forget, but the near-identical facial features and the same name now captivated his curiosity, and he needed to know what the pages within would reveal. Holding the book in both hands, he turned it over and read the synopsis printed on the back.

Feared by many, underestimated by few, and respected by all, Danny Wilson aka The Persuader, was the man called when dialogue was no longer effective.

From his humble beginnings in post-war Britain, to his rise to notoriety in London's East End, this is the story of how one man single-handedly created the intimidating image of the debt collector.

Packed full of first-hand anecdotes from family, friends and cohorts who ran with him, his story is one of crime and punishment from the depths of the East End, which ultimately ended in despair as Danny tried and failed to move on from a past that continued to haunt him.

The book was shaking in Danny's hands; hands that were clasped tightly around the cover as if it was one of his past victims. He could feel it flex within his grip. The description was too accurate, too specific to his own life.

A worrying thought crossed his mind, and he quickly surveyed the store, expecting to see a shadowy figure lurking in the corner, having dispatched the elderly owners by some grizzly means so they could be alone. But the place was empty. He glanced over his shoulder and out onto the street, believing that there would be a dark vehicle with blacked-out windows parked up. But the view was full of motorists and passersby unconcerned with the events unfolding within the quaint bookshop.

Turning around and seeing his chair in the corner of the store, he felt himself drawn to that leather-clad haunt. Negotiating the stacks of books and crowded shelves, he slumped down and prised open the biography, opting to begin at the start, so ensuring that no detail was missed, and this hoax, or trick, or whatever it was, would be revealed.

It began, as all biographies do, with his childhood. It was such a long time ago now. The country was still reeling from the war, ration books and rubble still featured heavily in day to day life. But this was nothing new, any historical account of that time would tell the same story. It was the details, however, that coloured this tale and drew Danny further into the spiral of confusion and mystery. They were indistinguishable from his life's history.

There were specifics such as his pet rat Toby that lived in a shoebox under his bed. His mother hated that rodent and emitted a shriek so loud when she first discovered him, that it caused the neighbours to rush in expecting the worst.

Or how he and his best friend Peter used to play in the alleyway between their homes. Childhood laughter was frequently heard throughout that brick-lined passage until one day, Peter wasn't allowed out any more. Several years passed before Danny learnt what polio was.

The parallel life story continued into his teenage years and his first kiss. Wendy Stafford was her name—auburn hair, hazel eyes and dense freckles that painted her soft face. It was in the park—between the dilapidated slide and a swing set that just consisted of hanging, limp chains, devoid of the seats that had rotted away years ago—that they kissed. Caught up in his pubescent emotions he thought it would be the start of something special, until he discovered that Wendy had done it as a dare. The news had crushed him, left him a weeping mess for days. He'd even contemplated suicide; such were the depths to which he'd fallen.

Now sat in the leather chair, Danny looked up from the book. He'd never told anyone about that. The other details could have been gleaned from family members or neighbours. But the thoughts of suicide had never been spoken aloud. For the first time in decades his palms began to sweat.

He continued to read, now up to his twenties and the turning point in his life. The fateful choice he'd made to earn a few extra shillings. He was just tagging along really. An extra pair of hands if things went south; which of course they did. He'd been in a few scraps growing up—who hadn't?—but his large size had kept him out of the worst of trouble. But that night, outnumbered and with his back against the wall, he became aware of what he was truly capable. The fight may have come to an end, but that didn't mean he was done with his assailants. The ones that got away were left disfigured, and subsequently spread warnings of The Persuader.

Danny took a moment to reflect on those screams and pleas for mercy. They'd not been offered much attention in these later years of his life; his mind now crowded with other unfortunate souls that shouted louder and fought harder for his attention. These same souls were now on the page before him, invading his peaceful solace. With each page turn a new victim was unveiled, complete with many of the gory details.

Danny didn't feel the bead of sweat roll off his temple, or the subtle vibrating of his right leg. He was too focused on how these final moments, which were shared between him, the victim and a particularly effective tool, were displayed here in black and white. He never spoke of his methods. Anyone who was familiar with them was either not in a position to meaningfully communicate anymore, or was decomposing at the landfill.

As he read his way towards the end of the biography, the final pages took on more of an obituary tone, similar to something that would be spoken aloud at a lonely funeral. With wide, panicked eyes, The Persuader spoke the final paragraph aloud:

For all the punishment and cruelty that Danny Wilson inflicted on others, ultimately, he was the most tortured victim. He spent his final years at a local bookshop, a place he visited every day, sat alone, attempting to escape his past. That was, until his past eventually found him. The End.

Danny stared intently at those final two words, trying to make sense of them, when he was interrupted by the chiming of the bell that hung above the entrance.

Mors Prope

...the scuffed and worn axe swung through the air, connecting with its intended victim at the point where the shoulder met the neck, just as Tobias' father had shown him when he was a boy. The Barrister armour was tough where it needed to be, but there were weaknesses if you knew where to aim.

The tarnished blade continued on its trajectory, burying itself deep into the damned soldier. It did not sever the head, but the man wouldn't be of concern any more. Tobias took another step forward and spun, momentarily turning his back to the attacking, thousand-strong army. As he did so, he crouched, avoiding the swing of a glistening sword that whooshed over him. Focusing the spinning inertia into his weapon, he drove it through the legs of the man who brandished the glistening sword. The bones popped like burning branches of the clan's campfire the night before.

Tobias heard a scream, but it was one of the dozens that surrounded him as other limbs and bodies fell to the sodden ground. Ground his family had farmed for generations. Ground he'd worked all of the thirty-two hard years of his existence. He knew which crops were best to plant just by the feel of the soil, even the taste of it. But that didn't matter anymore. It was useless now. It would take years of falling rain to cleanse the earth of what was happening today.

It was on this green, undulating land that his father had trained him. From a young age he was swinging an axe at a tree stump dressed in the regalia of the Barristers. It was like his father knew this day would come. Yet he would never see it, for his last moments were spent at the end of a rope, suspended by three men adorned with the same uniform as that battered and chipped old stump.

The Barrister tumbled to the ground, his shiny weapon at his side and hands splayed around what remained of his legs. Tobias didn't spare the man a thought as he burst up from his crouched position, swinging his axe upwards and into the jaw of another enemy. The fool was running towards Tobias as best as his cumbersome armour would allow, his sword held high, uncontrolled and uncoordinated. He was yelling something indiscernible that was lost to the cacophony of metal clashing and men dying. Tobias' axe barely slowed as it tore through the fool's helmet, flinging it into the air and silencing the man forever. The spray of blood spattered Tobias' painted face and blurred his vision. He blinked quickly in succession and rubbed his eyes with a hand bound in a glove made from rabbit skin. Rabbits that he and his father had snared together, the day before the Barristers visited their farm. Tobias' eyes narrowed at the memory. His focus returned in time to see a shimmering white light fill his vision...

... Fowler wasn't going to waste the opportunity. He'd just witnessed that Godless bastard take David from this earth, and he wouldn't let him die in vain. The two teenagers had grown up near the border, under the constant threat of the savages who crossed the ranges in search of deer. Deer that had belonged to Fowler and his family. They'd hunted wild beasts with their bare hands, roaming the forests like a pack of wolves. Devouring their prey where they fell. Everyone knew this. He and David had come across one such pack many moons ago. They'd hid amongst the undergrowth and listened as several wild-haired, dirty scavengers conversed in some pig dialect, their mouths and hands stained red from a fresh kill.

Fowler was afraid of them then, but not now. Not when they fell at his blade. Not when they'd taken his blood brother from him. The sharpened, silver sword sliced through another savage. The sight of the victim's eyes widening and the stream of red pouring from his gasping mouth fuelled Fowler's anguish. With each lunge and swipe of his weapon another wild-man fell. The image of his slain friend never left his mind. He would never see him again, and now he would make sure that this barbaric enemy suffered the same fate.

He was surrounded by a blur of conflict, and watched as one by one this plague succumbed to the power of the Almighty. He glanced up at the sun that hung against the brilliant blue sky. It shone down upon them as if pleased with their actions. Proud of their purge. It was then that he felt a pain in his side. It was hot and wet, like dripping wax. He was confronted with what appeared to be a crazed, hysterical woman. Long greasy hair was streaked across her face. The area around her eyes and mouth were painted black, making her appear like a menacing skull. She swiped at him again, her curved blade penetrating the connection between Fowler's breast and back plate, coming to a stop somewhere deep behind his ribs. His gasp at the searing pain turned to a gargled cry as the knife was twisted, churning his insides. The Medusa-like figure filled his vision, restricted by the confines of his helmet. She was screaming at him, as if possessed by the Devil. They truly were savages. She leapt up and wrapped her wiry arms and legs around him, encasing his body. He stumbled backwards, clattering to the ground. Sat on his chest, the Medusa raised her hands high into the air, letting out an unearthly shrill as she did so. Fowler felt his warm blood drip onto his face through the visor of his helmet, then the sensation of...

...Mary knelt over the pathetic soldier, stabbing him over and over. A viscous, crimson liquid spilled from the dented helmet. She knew he was dead. He was killed after the first blow. But she also knew others were watching. If these bastards wanted savages, then that's what they'd get. They'd invaded her home and had their way with her. She'd now have her way with them. She screamed as she'd screamed that fateful day, but this time the cry was full of venge...

...The feral creature's head was removed with ease. The commander barely broke his stride. He was surveying the battlefield before the thing's head was rolling across the red earth. His men were putting on a noble show. Their king would be proud. It was a shame that his earlier... persuasive methods had not swayed these animals, and that many of his men would come to an honourable end here today. But the king's law would be respected.

Through the thin slit of his helmet, the commander sighted his next victim. He marched towards it, his weighty armour clanking with each footstep. In his peripheral vision he saw another animal attempt an attack; its flimsy hammer—cobbled together from twine and a hunk of metal—ricocheted off his shoulder plate. The creature's roar morphed from fury to pain as the commander's engraved, ornate sword sliced through its belly, spilling entrails onto the ground. A lenient sentence for its crime, the commander mused.

He felt a weight on his back, then what felt like tentacles reach in under his helmet and begin to tug.

With a hefty, lumbering arm he swiped at the attacker, but to no avail. He spun on the spot, trying to throw the assailant off, but the tugging continued. The helmet started to move, sliding up his sweat-covered face. With his sword at his side, he gripped at the helmet with his free hand, but the metal-plated glove restricted his dexterity. Inch by inch it was lifted, with the commander rocking from side to side, until finally it was flung from his head, and the thing responsible for its removal fell to the ground.

The stale atmosphere of the helmet interior was replaced with the fetid stench of death. It was a scent he'd never grown accustomed to. It stained his nostrils and coated the back of his throat. Raising his sword, he turned and scowled at whoever was foolish enough to attack him. He was met by a small boy, maybe ten or eleven years old. His soft features and startling blue eyes reminded the commander of his son, who waited for his return once this final conquest, was over. He stared down at the child. His grip relaxed around his weapon and it fell to his side...

...Evan watched the arrow leave his bow and sail over the carnage, eventually striking its target between the eyes. He smiled to himself as the metal-clad soldier collapsed in a heap, and reached down for another arrow. The tensioned string quivered between his fingers as he peered down the sight and across the unfolding conflict. His aim was true, having spent his life hunting on these lands. Lands his ancestors had presided over, cared for, and which were now being ravished by this invading threat. Evan watched his brothers and sisters fight bravely, knowing that the gathering around the campfire would be smaller tonight. Seeing another exposed enemy, he took a deep breath and tensed his body, ensuring that no arrow was wasted.

The sound of galloping rose above the roar of mutilation before him. It increased in intensity, the approaching thunder interspersed with the unmistakable groans of war horses being pushed to their limit.

Evan spun around to be greeted by a charging cavalry. His mouth fell open at the sight of it. The poised arrow flew uselessly into the air, over the tops of the galloping hooves that engulfed him...

...hot breath bellowed from Steeler's flared nostrils. Forced on by his master, the humans fell below him like a scythe through a cornfield. Through his iron-plated hooves he felt bones snap and shatter. But still his master did not relent; unconcerned with the unstable ground or the plight of his fellow-kind. It was not always like this. They had run before, together, through green open fields with no other humans in sight. At a time when his master was kind.

Steeler felt pain across his powerful, black body. Tight areas of heat burned with the flexing of his muscles. The blistering pain spread and grew, becoming more intense as it did so. Suddenly, something exploded inside of him, launching him up...

...the thick pike that Bartholomew held disappeared into the body of the charging beast. He watched as the rider was flung from the saddle and plummeted into the depths of the ensuing chaos. But the slain horse bucked and kicked out, falling onto its side before Bartholomew was able to move away. It was impossible to resist the weight of the steed, and it crushed Bartholomew's legs and torso as it fell. The initial flash of agony was replaced with an icy panic at the realisation that he was pinned, unable to move, with the air being slowly squeezed from his lungs. This was no way for him to go. He was a kind, caring man. He should never have left his peaceful home. His wife was sick, their children too young.

Footsteps approached, pulling Bartholomew's attention back to the present. He was facing the other way, unable to turn to see who it was. Maybe it was a fellow clansman, coming to his aid, saving him from this plight. He would be carried home, back to the hills and fields of his childhood, and his loving family of five.

Something was muttered in a language Bartholomew didn't understand, and a cold implement was dragged across his neck...

"That's for Steeler," Marcus said, wiping the knife across his tunic. The knife was a gift from...

Broken Arrow (Intermission)

A clenched fist grabs at the plaid tablecloth. The finely groomed bachelor slips from his chair, taking the overpriced wine, filet mignon and candles, with him.

The crash of glass and crockery startles the pianist, bringing the ambient music to an abrupt halt. It is immediately replaced by the hysterical scream of the attractive brunette who was also eating at the table, but is now struggling to stand in her new heels as her date writhes around on the posh carpet.

The man claws at his chest with his free hand. His mouth opens and closes like a freshly caught fish.

A waiter appears dressed in an ill-fitting suit. The tray of hors d'oeuvres he carried is cast aside as he drops down beside the man. With intertwined hands he begins rhythmically pressing down on the stricken diner while mouthing the lyrics to Night Fever by the Bee Gees.

"It's Stayin Alive!" a voice yells.

"Damn it, I'm trying," the waiter replies. He pinches the diner's nose and expels two lungfuls of life-giving air. The man's torso expands by worrisome proportions. The sight elicits a series of gasps from the other patrons.

"Someone, call an ambulance," another voice shouts, presumably belonging to someone not in possession of a mobile phone.

The flustered waiter resumes singing in a distracted tone as the compressions restart. "Night fever, night fever..."

The kitchen doors burst open. A defibrillator appears, held within the outstretched hands of a stout chef while she shouts,   "He's having a heart attack."

The announcement whips up another round of gasps from the guests who watch from the safety of their tables.

The chef slides in alongside the patient. The singing waiter is usurped from the scene midway through the second verse. A charged paddle is wielded in each hand. "Clear!"

The near-cadaver spasms from the shock of a thousand volts.

"I'm losing him! Clear!"

The body jolts again. The defibrillator is discarded and heavy fists rain down on an unbeating heart. "I can't do this alone."

The brunette in the new heels drops to her knees and pounds at her date's chest. The waiter is soon at her side and the three of them beat the corpse to the butchered melody of the Bee Gees.

Meanwhile, high up on the rafters, out of sight of anyone who would care to look, sit two cherubs. One slowly lowers a bow, the arrow recently let loose. His old face, now more prune than plum, is twisted in a combination of surprise and horror.

The other flicks away the butt of a cigarette. An eye-patch is strapped over the left side of his furrowed face. "Damn it, Steve. You've done it again."

"It's not my fault. These arrows don't fly straight."

"Ah, you've been pedalling that excuse since the Renaissance." A pair of dishevelled wings flutters into life. "Come on; let's get out of here before Death turns up."

Trophy Hunter

(First published on The Other Stories podcast, May 2020)

"Already? I swear it takes more and more of this stuff to put you boys down." The voice is female and speaks matter-of-factly. Save for a mass of blonde hair, Tyler's vision is too blurry to make out any other details. He can smell perfume, hairspray and leather.

The voice continues, "You know they use this stuff in game reserves where you're not allowed to kill the animals anymore. They tranquilise the rhinos and giraffes long enough for hunters to get a photo before they wake up and stumble back into the bush."

Tyler blinks several times, but his vision remains distorted. His world swirls as though at sea. He tries to move from his slouched position, but his limbs are unresponsive. He attempts to ask where he is, who this woman is, what's going on, but the gag prevents the questions from escaping.

The woman ignores the muffled words. "They say it's more humane, but I'm not sure how humane it is having a park full of doped up wildlife." She holds up a syringe and flicks it a few times while she speaks. The sight of the hypodermic needle turns Tyler's muffled words into muffled cries. "Oh please, I very much doubt you're unfamiliar with these."

Tyler shakes his head in a futile attempt to prevent the needle from being plunged into his neck. It does little. Blurry colours merge to black.

A mechanical whirring welcomes Tyler back to reality. He is weightless, no, suspended. His wrists and ankles are now restrained, bound together as though he is being transported by some cannibal tribe. The artificial light is too bright; his eyes remain as slits, limiting the details around him. He can make out the chain from which he hangs. He slowly rotates until his head knocks into something hard and metallic.

"Whoops, sorry about that," the woman says. Her voice is familiar, but Tyler can't place it. "Shouldn't leave a mark. Would hate to damage the goods on your big day."

The impact kick-starts Tyler's awareness. He tilts his head back and views the world from an inverted position. He is in a garage. Shelves line walls full of boxes and tins. Garden tools are leant up underneath. He realises that he'd knocked his head against a windscreen while being hoisted out of a red convertible. He knows this car, but from where? More of the garage comes into view, including the operator of the engine block. It's her, the driver from the hotel. The memories rush back all at once...

He was in his plush hotel suite. While waiting for another coat of fake tan to dry, he perused the selection of thongs laid out across the bed. It was a toss-up between sparkly gold or classic blue. Behind him the sun was setting; the bright city lights becoming ever more vivid. The phone had rung, his driver was downstairs. A glance at the clock revealed that the driver was early. Tyler slammed the phone down and marched into the bathroom to grab the hairdryer. The tan set in minutes. The third coat would have to wait. He manoeuvred himself into the blue thong—classic blue was always a winner—and slung on the complementary XXX-Large robe.

The waiting driver was a petite blonde woman, dressed in a navy chauffeur uniform and all dolled up as though she was attending a high stakes fundraiser at the Hamptons. Her name tag read: Simone. She met him with a fake smile and took his bags to the awaiting vehicle. He expected a Limo or Benz, but instead a sporty red convertible greeted him, roof down, waxed to a high sheen. Simone stuffed his bags into the limited boot space while he climbed into the back seat. The vehicle rocked from side to side, struggling under his bulk. Thankfully it was only a short drive to the venue. He'd be having words with the organisers upon his arrival. From up front, Simone prattled on about the importance of hydration, especially with the recent humid weather. She reached into a cooler and handed back a chilled bottle of water. He cracked open the seal and took a sip, mainly as an attempt to shut her up. Simone watched him in the rear-view mirror. The water tasted off and left a bitter aftertaste. That was his last thought before everything went dark and he awoke to the peculiar hunting practices of certain game reserves.

The whirring of the engine hoist comes to a stop. Tyler remains suspended above the vehicle. The gag continues to suppress his cries. With a grunt, Simone pushes the mechanism across the stone floor. The jolt causes Tyler to swing like the hanging balls of a Newton's Cradle. He is steered helplessly towards an open door that leads up a ramp and into a hallway.

The sedative is wearing off. Tyler can feel his muscles tingle as the sensation returns. The fogginess shrouding his mind clears, his vision sharpens. He can make out a ceiling filled with dusty chandeliers and cobwebs. Abstract artworks are hung on the walls. Between the canvases are stuffed heads of exotic animals—rhino, lion, and cheetah. A whole safari's worth watching a prizewinning, bound and gagged bodybuilder at the mercy of a woman a quarter his size.

"You like our collection? We preserve only the best specimens," Simone says with some pride. She doesn't allow Tyler the chance of a muffled reply before he is swiftly turned through ninety degrees and trundled into a library. He is abandoned in the centre of the room, while his tormentor busies herself with something out of sight. Tyler's wild eyes scan the library from his upside-down position. He's surrounded by dusty books and old tomes. A mahogany desk is to his left, a fireplace to his right with a framed photograph sitting on the mantelpiece. Craning his neck, he makes out an ageing man with an attractive blonde woman in his arms. Covered in liver spots and wrinkled skin, the man wears a matching khaki shirt and pants, and a pith helmet sitting at a slight angle. Mounted above the mantelpiece, a mighty lion head roars.

A mechanical shunt and grinding of gears snaps Tyler back to the present. The bookcase adjacent to the fireplace starts to move. A succession of ceiling lights bursts into life, illuminating a narrow corridor.

"I know what you're thinking," Simone says, now standing at Tyler's side. "What's with all the animals? I have my late husband to thank for that. Despite his many flaws, especially when it came to his attitude towards women, he knew his stuff when it came to taxidermy, I'll give him that. I've always struggled to get the eyes right. Anyway..."

They descend a short distance to a roller door. The bookcase grinds back into position, sealing them inside. Tyler sizes up Simone out of the corner of his eye; she would be no match for him on a level playing field. The possibility of escape causes adrenaline to flow through his system, washing away the lingering effects of the sedative. He would only need a second. Simone taps a series of numbers into an electronic keypad, making no effort to hide it. Tyler memorises the code, capitalising on her carelessness. He suppresses a sly grin.

The roller door winds itself up. The area beyond is shrouded in darkness. The corridor lighting that seeps in does little to reveal what lies in wait. With some effort, Simone pushes Tyler into the centre of the room. "I'll leave you boys to get acquainted while I slip into something more appropriate."

Footsteps disappear into the darkness. Tyler is left suspended. He pushes Simone's strange comment aside. This is his chance. He fights against the restraints, muscles tensed. The engine hoist rocks back and forth. If he can just topple it over...

A distant flick of a switch floods the area with light. The escape is momentarily halted as Tyler winces against the glare. Arching and twisting his back, he can take in more and more of the room. The excitement of a possible escape turns to sickening dread. He now realises why the code was not hidden from view; he's underestimated his captor.

In one corner of the large windowless room is a living area, tastefully decorated as if it was still nineteen seventy-two. A floral sofa is angled towards a TV, a shag rug placed on the floor. Sat on the sofa, dressed in only a thong, is the unmoving, bulging physique of Jay Francis. A previous winner of Mr Olympia, he went missing several years ago. It appears he's been here all along, angled at the TV with a remote control in one hand and the other resting along the back of the sofa. An unsettling smile is fixed upon his tanned face, made more so by the pair of plastic googly eyes that rest in his eye sockets.

In another corner is a pink tiled bathroom, complete with shower cubicle, sink, toilet and old bodybuilding rival Flex Bridges. He retired back in oh-eight. At least, that's what the world thought. But now he is stuck in place, his muscular arm raised up, squeegee in hand, destined to forever clean shower glass. He grins tirelessly despite the grim prospect, the wide googly eyes resting at a cock-eyed angle.

The third corner is a simple kitchenette, complete with cupboards and two gas burners. The oven door is open, and bending over it is multiple Mr Universe-winner, Toby Gillingham. His ripped figure—covered in only an apron, thong and oven mitts—is removing a tray of baked goods. A smug smile is etched upon his frozen face as he permanently looks back over his shoulder. One of Toby's googly eyes has come away, leaving a dark cavity in the left side of his face.

In the final corner is a double bed, complete with side tables and lamps. The bed is empty, the patterned sheets pulled tight.

A grand recess is built into one of the walls, the details within remain covered in shadow. Another flick of a switch and bulbs strung around an ornate arch begin to rhythmically blink into life. Standing below is a fleshy statue of a man, a victim of time and age. He is dressed in a dark suit, his wrinkled mouth half-open, and his plastic eyes unfocused. In one hand an open book rests, facing upward upon spread fingers. The other arm is raised out, as though addressing a congregation. Tyler recognises the man. He tries his best to pull himself around, twisting against the restraints to get a better look. Yes, he was in the photo upstairs, dressed in the hunting uniform.

The sound of wheels trundling across the polished wooden flooring catches Tyler's attention. He arches himself around and comes to realise that the human mannequins of this place are not static but mounted on dollies. More concerning is that Simone has ditched the chauffeur uniform for a tattered wedding dress. The once-classy garment is now stained; the absence of flower girls causes the train to drag across the floor.

One by one she lines the bodybuilders up. Jay fixed in the seated position, remote in hand. Flex standing straight and reaching up with a squeegee. Toby bent over, holding a tray of mouldy cakes. All of them are in thongs, their veiny muscles bulging, while unnaturally large grins and fake eyes fill their faces. Unseen speakers start to play a bridal chorus.

The bride arrives at Tyler's side and begins to shove her strung-up husband-to-be down the aisle. The celebrant and congregation greet them. Behind the celebrant, stacked on top of each other against the back wall, are the preserved bodies of several scantily clad women. They all look like Simone: slim, blonde, petite. Their skin the colour of distressed leather. A pile of tarnished trophies gathering dust.

Simone notices Tyler eying up the human pile. "You'll have to excuse the mess. They're my late husband's collection. I've not got around to clearing them away yet." She takes a quick breath and composes herself. Tyler is forced to watch as she nods along with something unsaid by the celebrant. A bouquet is held at Simone's waist, and at one point she removes her hand and flaps it in front of her, attempting to banish any falling tears. Finally, she says, "I do."

Tyler's eyes widen. He begins to writhe around on the end of the engine block, an animal caught in a snare. Simone waits patiently. At one point she turns and smiles apologetically to the grinning congregation. Tyler's thrashing continues for another minute before he is overcome with futility. His muscles relax, drained from the fight. His soon-to-be wife turns to the celebrant and says, "He does."

Simone wipes a tear away. She kneels down, pecks Tyler on the cheek, and asks, "So, which side of the bed do you prefer?"

The Pieces Shall be Ordered

"What the hell was that?" Darren rubbed his sore eyes. The lights dimmed again. The air conditioners ground to a halt and computer screens went black. For a brief moment he caught his reflection in the dark monitor; his hair ruffled, his face drawn. "Bloody C-Unit and their load tests." The power returned kick-starting hundreds of electrical devices throughout the office.

Darren glanced at the clock: six-fifteen. He let out a weary sigh which morphed into a cough. He'd passed on Friday drinks to go home early and try to recover from this worsening illness, yet was somehow still at his desk. And now there were notifications to deal with, dozens of them popping up and crowding his screen. "Yes, I'm aware of the power surge, thank you." It wasn't possible to close the message boxes as quickly as they appeared.

"Everything all right?" Liz asked, peering over the cubicle wall. Her frizzy blonde hair was tied back, revealing a pair of bright jangling earrings. A hectic week of work had worn down her usual smiling demeanour.

"What? Yeah... fine." Darren tilted his head upwards, cradling it in hands. "Just... this thing."

"You need to go home," Liz said. "You look as bad as your desk."

Darren resisted the urge to survey the surrounding clutter. He didn't need reminding of another pending job on the To-Do list. "I will, just need to find out what C-Unit has been up to."

Liz frowned. "C-Unit? The bio-printing wing? They shut down months ago."

Darren's blank face stared back, partly due to his obliviousness to this fact, and partly due to tiredness.

"Do you not read your email... never mind," Liz continued. "Management diverted funding to the guys working on that AI programme. Jericho or Geronimo. I dunno. The one tasked with bringing about world peace."

The ache behind Darren's eyes increased. "You're taking the piss, right?"

"This is what happens when you let liberals take the wheel."

Darren let the comment slide. He wasn't in the mood to debate politics or the confusing logic of a military contractor researching world peace via AI. "I thought C-Unit had cracked this DNA printing thing, or whatever it was they were doing with stem cells, or something..."

Liz shrugged. "Who knows what they were doing in there. All a bit academic now anyway. They weren't delivering so they got the chop. And so will you if you stay here any longer."

Taking the hint, Darren switched off the monitor, thankful to escape the growing list of notifications. They would still be there on Monday. "Night, Liz." He grabbed his jacket off the back of the chair and headed to the lifts.

"Feel better," Liz called back.

Darren grimaced to himself, wishing it was that simple. He zipped up the jacket, and as he did so, noticed out of the corner of his eye a security camera tracking him as he walked. Stepping into the lift, he saw that it remained trained on him, a red light blinking under the lens. They locked stares for the briefest of moments. Then the camera swivelled away as though spotted. The doors closed on an uneasy expression.

The station was the usual hive of disarray as commuters fought for position on the platform. The approaching train ground to a stop and the doors whooshed open, signalling the chaos to begin. Disembarking passengers fought against the tide of elbows and grunts as they attempted to flee the carriage. With shoulders slung low, Darren joined the war zone, knowing that the next train would be as bad.

The closing doors squeezed together the bodies of strangers. Darren felt breath on the back of his neck. He screwed up his eyes and wished himself away, but his sinuses had alternative plans. His nose tickled, his mouth arched. A sneeze was brewing. He battled against his pinned arms, desperate to shield the others from the inevitable spray of infection, but it was futile. The posture of the person beside him tightened. The pressure of the bodies around him lessened. No one said anything, but he felt their scowls for the remainder of the commute.

Upon his release, he trod up a flight of stairs that led to the high street. With his head lowered and arms pressed deep into his pockets, he did his best to avoid others who shared the pavement and soon arrived at the ugly concrete high-rise that he called home. He was asleep within minutes of turning the key in the door.

**

Saturday morning sunlight poured through a large gap in the bedroom curtains. Darren's eyes burned at the sight of it, his head throbbed from the glare. The illness had firmly taken hold. Prising himself from the bed, he shuffled across unhoovered carpet and past piles of clothes, into the kitchen. The stack of dirty dishes and accompanying flies went ignored. The kettle was flicked on. Sugary tea would make everything better. He zoned out while staring out of the window of the fourteenth-floor flat. The view over the city was vast, comprised of countless terraced houses extending to the horizon. The occasional church spire or grey supermarket roof broke up the monotony. In the foreground was the local park bustling with kids and dog walkers. The click of the kettle brought him back to reality. As he turned, he noticed a spider's web in the corner of the window. It had been there for some time, but he never remembered it looking like this. Instead of the silky strands spiralling out in concentric circles, it was composed of squares. He stared at it for a moment longer, then with a shake of the head, reached for a mug.

Unable to face the thought of leaving the house, the day was wasted away via a combination of movies and social media scrolling. The snug embrace of the sofa was abandoned only for bathroom breaks or cups of tea. By the time evening arrived he felt mentally prepared to indulge in some comfort food. A pan of chicken soup warmed on the oven top. The dirty dishes remained for another day, yet the flies were noticeably absent. Perhaps they'd fallen victim to the geometric web which had now grown in size?

While the soup simmered, he saw a straight formation of migrating birds soar across the red and orange sky. His eyes narrowed. *Didn't they usually travel in a V-shape?* He carried the pan of soup back to the sofa. As the thirty-eighth season of Big Bang Theory started to roll, Darren noticed that the flies had relocated. Arranged in a three by three grid on the wall behind the TV, they moved as one, walking across the peeling wallpaper. Upon reaching the other side, they turned ninety degrees, moved down three fly lengths and continued back the other way. A faint trail of yellow was left in their wake, barely noticeable in the dim lighting. The soup and TV went ignored as Darren stared in fascination at the display. *Maybe the bugs were ill too?* He definitely needed more sleep.

Sunday morning sunlight lit up the bedroom. Darren stretched, his muscles already feeling looser. His nose was sore but not streaming as before, and the fogginess of his mind seemed to have burned away. The coughing remained however, his lungs feeling stuffy and dusty like a neglected attic.

Repeating the actions of the previous morning, but this time with more vigour, he flicked the kettle on intending to fix some coffee. While the water bubbled away, he stacked the dirty dishes to the side. He noticed that the spider web had evolved into something resembling a dodecahedron. The strands had a curious yellow tint to them. The cupboards were devoid of coffee; a strong tea was no substitute. A walk to the local cafe and some fresh air would do him good anyway.

He strolled through the park. He frowned at the sight of the morning joggers all running at the same speed, their legs moving in sync. Dogs remained silently at their owners' sides, no sticks were thrown. Even the ducks bobbing about on the water were arranged as a matrix. They moved much like the flies had done the night before.

Darren's pace quickened. Upon entering the cafe, he felt a sense of relief as he saw the area packed with punters. He joined the queue and realised that the usual hubbub of chatter and gossip was absent. The occasional cough cut through the silence. A glance around the room revealed the table and chairs arranged as a grid, with the patrons all sitting in the same position, legs crossed and leaning in, resting on their elbows.

"What is going...?" His muttering was interrupted by a bout of coughing. The itchiness in his lungs was becoming more bothersome. The entire room turned to look at him, then sipped from their coffee cups in an almost choreographed manner.

Darren ran his hands down his face. "No, no, no..." He abandoned the queue, and under the watchful gaze of rows of birds perfectly lined up along the power lines, retreated to his flat. The spider web had developed into complicated 3D cubes. It was cleared away without regard. The flies that continued on their march across the walls were dispatched with fly spray. The yellow powdery trail was washed from the walls. The dishes were scrubbed clean, the clothes tidied. All the while, the coughing continued.

**

Monday morning sunlight shone into the bedroom. Darren struggled to leave the bed. Not because of any lingering flu symptoms—he felt awake and alert—but because of what strangeness possibly awaited him today.

Leaving the sanctuary of the flat, he slowly stepped out onto the street. Nothing was out of place. Cars cruised by in an orderly fashion. People passed without issue. Darren cautiously entered the train station and prepared himself for the carnage of the daily commute. However, everything was calm and peaceful. There was no bottleneck at the ticket barriers. Commuters lined up on the platform in rows, patiently waiting for the arriving train. Darren fought the urge to join the furthest queue and chose to observe the curious spectacle from a distance. He remained on the periphery until the train arrived. There were no elbows, no collisions, and no hassle, simply a dignified and regimented exchange of people. He joined the procession, moving as though on a conveyor belt, and for the first time enjoyed a civilised commute with ample personal space.

Walking through the office, tracked under the watchful gaze of the security camera, he passed co-workers sat motionless in their spotless cubicles, one hand on the mouse, the other at the keyboard. They stared transfixed at the computer screens.

Liz approached, her frizzy hair now straightened, the jangling earrings replaced with single golden studs. The Friday afternoon expression of weariness had turned into a glazed-over passiveness.

"Morning, Liz," Darren said. The greeting went unacknowledged as she strode past. "Oookay."

Arriving at his disorderly desk, Darren resisted the need to tidy away the loose papers and stained coffee cups. Pens remained strewn across the workspace, his mind focused on the slew of notifications that needed addressing. The computer monitor was switched on. There were more messages than he remembered, all relating to the electrical surge in C-Unit.

Opening up the power usage readings from the weekend, it appeared as though Friday evening's spike was the first in a series. Darren leant toward the monitor, struggling to make sense of the information. After a succession of clicks, he pulled up the CCTV recordings for the supposedly decommissioned lab. His mouth fell open. He stared in amazement as a fleet of drones ferried something from the bio-printer to the exhaust chute. He zoomed in and saw that a yellow pollen-like substance was being churned out and promptly whisked away by the buzzing devices. The substance was worryingly familiar, but a more pressing matter bothered him. Darren leant back into the chair. "Who's piloting the drones?"

He reached for the phone with the intent of speaking to upper management when the video footage of C-Unit closed down. "What the hell?"

A notification appeared in its place, different from the previous ones. It read: *The pieces shall be ordered. Jericho.*

"Jericho? Who is...the AI...?"

Another notification popped up. *To achieve peace, the pieces shall be ordered. Jericho.*

The unexpected statement triggered another coughing fit. Little was done to mitigate the spray of phlegm; such was Darren's stunned state. After a few short breaths, he composed himself. The phone receiver was returned. He wiped down the desk as instructed, his actions automatic as though controlled by another. He didn't notice the spots of yellow that peppered the spatters of mucus. In fact, he didn't notice much at all.

The Swing

Everyone is familiar with the sound of a squeaky swing. The high-pitched resonance that forces the listener to wince if it is allowed to continue unabated. You may have heard it the last time you took your kid to the playground, or while walking your dog through the park. Or even dredging up forgotten memories of an age when you enjoyed the simple pleasure of swinging back and forth.

At twenty past midnight, that's where the irritable noise should remain—as a memory. But not tonight. It's been going on like this for, I dunno, an hour at least. I should say something. If Janie were here, she would have told me to say something. She thought that it was a blessing that the rear garden backed onto a playground. "Less than ten seconds from dinner table to climbing frame," the estate agent had assured us. It was more like ten minutes once Janie and I had gathered together all of Patrick's stuff and he'd finally put his shoes and socks on.

A headache is already brewing. I roll over on the bed. The other side is just as uncomfortable and offers no improvement on the current situation.

There is a pair of earplugs somewhere, bought when we were replacing the bathroom. They were for Patrick. The purchase was such a rookie mistake. Getting foam buds into a two-year-old's ears was a nightmare. We went back to the hardware store the same day and got some ear defenders instead. God, he looked adorable in them.

The continued squeaking claws for my attention and pulls me from the sweet memory. Blood rushes to my muscles. The bed covers are torn off and my feet land heavily on the carpeted floor.

I march to the window. The curtains are pulled apart with such force that one of the runners springs free and sails across the room. I don't see where it lands. My attention is focused on the solitary figure stood in the playground. Dressed in a long black overcoat, the hood pulled up, the shadowy character pushes a vacant swing seat back and forth. The squeaking seems to increase in intensity.

I look for any others that might be in the park; drunks or teenagers with no better place to go. Yet the playground is empty. There is no one hanging around on the slide or resting on the seesaw. This isn't the suburb for that kind of thing anyway, the house prices see to that. The only alcoholics around here are the stay-at-home mums knocking back a bottle of overpriced vino every night.

The lonely figure is almost hidden in the darkness, absorbed by night, and would have gone unnoticed at a casual glance if it were not for the movement of the swing and the accompanying wail.

I bang on the window with a fist. The pane of glass rattles within the frame.

The figure does not react. The swing does not slow in its trajectory.

I try again, more forceful this time. My knuckles sting from the impact.

Nothing.

"Right," I spit. I go to open the window but it is caught on the latch. The damn thing sticks. We'd meant to sort it out. It was on the To-Do list that Janie and I are destined never to complete.

My attention is diverted to the infernal mechanism as I battle with the lever. It jolts to the side and I shunt the window upwards. As I do so I look back into the park. The figure is gone. No doubt scared off by the impending confrontation.

A satisfied smile grows across my face. I reach for the curtains and notice that the swing is motionless, just like the others around it.

**

"Mother-fucker." I grab a fistful of duvet and whip it off the bed. It flies off like a ship's sail caught in a storm. I'm at the window in a flash, the curtain flung back with similar intensity. The figure is there again, wearing the same stupid jacket and pushing the same empty swing that emits that irritating metal on metal cry. My furious eyes remain fixed on him as the window is forced open. There is no fumbling with the latch, and no chance for this inconsiderate prick to make an escape while I'm momentarily distracted.

The swing continues to glide back and forth, forced into action by two hands attached to a docile owner.

"'Scuse me, mate." I'm leaning out the window, ensuring that my voice is a little louder.

The figure doesn't react.

The swing replies instead in the only way it knows how.

"Oi, dickhead," I try again.

Not even a flinch.

I pull my body back into the dimly-lit bedroom. "Right then." Socks are snatched from the wash basket, slippers retrieved from under the bed. Wrapping a chequered dressing gown around myself, I'm out of the bedroom and starting down the landing. I pass Patrick's room and pound down the stairs. The carpet does little to soften the footfalls. I'm through the kitchen and at the back door. From here I can see the tops of the playground equipment; the launch of the slide, the thin edges of the climbing frame and the upper outline of the swings. All of the chains are still, save one that shrieks and wails in the night.

Six strides through the unkempt rear garden and I'm at the hinged panel we built into the fence. The sliding bolt that secures the entranceway—positioned high up so that Patrick couldn't reach it—is showing signs of rust. Creepers have begun to grow around it, claiming it as their own.

There is a throbbing in my temples, my legs feel weak. I attempt to shift the bolt across, but it refuses to move.

The swing yells out in what sounds like taunting laughter.

I shoulder the fence panel in response, remembering that it needed to be weighted to allow the bolt to move. An additional security measure that would have had its benefits once Patrick was old enough to reach the latch. But now it acts as an infuriating obstacle that needs to be overcome.

I launch my whole bodyweight at the wooden entranceway; it flexes from the impact. The bolt jumps out of the holster and slides back with a loud bang. I lean back and pull open the panel, announcing my arrival in the most dramatic fashion possible.

I'm greeted with an empty playground.

The swing is still. The night is silent.

I scan the area, eyes narrowed, checking that no one is watching from the bushes. I listen out for the sound of escaping footfalls.

Nothing.

Approaching the stationary swing, forcing back the memories it invokes, I stand where the figure once did. The chunk of moulded plastic appears so innocuous. A shaking hand is raised and the swing pushed. There is no shriek, no shrill, no cry. It moves as I remember, minus the child's laughter I miss so much.

The playground is scanned a final time. I clear my throat, straighten my posture, and head back to the house. The entranceway through the fence is wide open, as is the back door. My stomach flips at the realisation. I quickly survey the house. The bedroom window is ajar. The curtains that shield Patrick's room from the outside world are drawn, as they have remained for the past several months.

Prising myself from the spot, I head toward the house, my attention on the back door. Something flickers above in my peripheral vision. Did the curtain in Patrick's room move? It was probably nothing. Wind or something. But on this still night, the increasing sickness in my gut suggests otherwise.

The entranceway through the fence is closed but not locked. The back door is left in a similar manner. Moving through the kitchen, I stop at the counter littered with empty whisky bottles. The top drawer is eased open and I remove the largest of the kitchen knives on offer— the Gyutou Chef Knife. One of the more useful wedding presents we were gifted.

I creep into the hallway, taking care not to disturb the creaking floorboards, and arrive at the base of the stairs. All is quiet. An attempt at swallowing fails due to a dry and coarse throat.

The grip around the Chef Knife is adjusted. It's held out as if I'm about to cut a wedding cake. Memories of that magical day Janie and I shared are pushed aside. I need to focus. With my back pressed against the wall, I take the stairs one slow step at a time. Over the thudding of my heart, I tell myself that I'm acting irrationally. Yet the knife is not lowered, and every effort is made not to alert a possible intruder of my approach.

I'm on the landing. Framed photos of a smiling family hang on the walls. Patrick's room is on the right. The door is open. As it always is. It was how he left it. I sneak up across the landing—it feels narrower and more claustrophobic than before—and arrive at the entrance to my son's room. I lick dry lips; count to three, and move on four. My neck cranes around the door frame. The room is empty. Of course it is. There are few places to hide. Under the bed is full of boxes. The cupboard is split into shelves that even Patrick struggled to conceal himself within, during games of hide and seek.

I convince myself that I don't need to step inside and investigate further. Satisfied, I move on to the bathroom. Towels are heaped on the floor; the leaky tap that I've still not got around to fixing, continues to drip. But nothing is out of the ordinary. I'm alone. Everything is back to how it should be.

Returning to a cold bed, I attempt to sleep with an eight-inch blade under the pillow.

**

I saw the figure again today. On the way back from the hardware store. I'd just purchased a tin of oil, can of CRC and a set of bolt cutters for good measure. As I drove past the park the figure was there, stood in broad daylight, surrounded by oblivious children playing under the watchful supervision of their parents. No one paid him any attention as the empty swing continued to be pushed back and forth. From this new vantage, I should have been able to make out a face, but the shadow the hood cast created a deep void that swallowed up the light. The figure did not look up, did not acknowledge my presence and did not allow the swing to come to a rest. But my plan would soon see that change.

**

It's twilight when I leave the house and head to the rear gate, bolt cutters in hand. After much deliberation over a tumbler of cheap scotch, it was decided that oiling the chains would simply be a temporary fix, a band-aid over an infected wound. The swing needed to be removed, the limb needed to be amputated.

The playground is empty. In the fading light I take the bolt cutters to the chains, snipping them off at the very top. There was to be no option of fixing the play set, no chance of retaliation. The first chain falls to the ground and coils up like an injured snake. The second soon follows, crashing to the ground in a metallic jumble. The evidence of the vandalism is stuffed into my pack. I consider leaving it as a message. No, leaving it as a warning. A warning that I am not to be messed with, that I am capable of taking matters into my own hands. But instead, I choose to remove the seat and chains, so hindering the chances of repair.

I return to the house with the slightest spring in my step. The bag is dropped down, the bolt cutters are leant against the counter, and the latest bottle of scotch picked up. The tumbler is refilled with a victory measure, and the living room sofa welcomes me back.

The room is bathed in the dull glow of the TV when I stir from a drunken slumber. The sharp tang of alcohol hangs in the air. A glance over the side of the sofa confirms that I must have dropped the glass when I passed out. It is another recent addition to the messy patchwork of stains that covers the floor. Soon after moving in, Janie insisted that the garish mint-green carpet was replaced with an overpriced 'stormy grey' number.

Peeling myself from the sofa, I wobble my way into the kitchen and rinse the empty glass in the sink. It is then filled, and I knock back several mouthfuls of tepid water in a vain attempt to soften the inevitable headache tomorrow. The tops of the playground equipment are visible in the moonlight. It is possible to make out the hanging chains of all the swings, bar one. "Damn right," I mutter. My dulled senses do not notice the slurred words or the slight sway to my stance. The tumbler is refilled. I go to leave the kitchen, and then it happens.

That despised metallic shriek forces itself back into my world.

I spin on the spot. A concentrated fury pumps through my veins.

The tumbler is launched at the back door and it explodes into thousands of glistening pieces that scatter across the tiled ground. Before they come to rest the bolt cutters are already within my firm grip. The door is yanked open.

I don't feel the shards of glass bury themselves deeper into the soles of my feet with each purposeful step.

I don't feel the long grass under my bleeding feet.
I don't feel the fresh night air against my skin.

All I feel is rage. The bolt cutters will not be used on the chains tonight.

The entranceway through the fence is pulled open and the sight awaiting stuns me to an abrupt halt.

The park is empty.

The play equipment is motionless.

The gap, where the offending swing once hung, remains. Yet the high-pitched cry continues to mock me. It then dawns on me that the source is not from the playground, but from within the house.

I look back at our once-perfect, two-bedroom detached home with its new bathroom, stormy-grey carpet and son's bedroom I'd not entered since they left. I then notice that the curtains to that hallowed room have been pulled back. A racing pulse hammers at my temples. Deep breaths launch spittle from my lips.

I'm at the house in seconds, at the base of the stairs in the blink of an eye. A trail of bloody footprints is left in my wake. There is no hesitation, no concern for creaky floorboards, no second thought given to the intruder who has made the mistake of crossing me. The stairs are taken three at a time. The metallic shrieking intensifies with each step. Shards are driven further into the soft flesh of my feet. The pain isn't comparable to what I'm about to inflict.

In the four strides it takes to reach Patrick's room the bolt cutters are raised up in attack. My arms shake in anticipation. I launch into the room, the significance of the action lost to the seething moment of anger.

The figure is stood, frozen in place, in the centre of the room. Dressed in that familiar long jacket, the raised hood shrouding its face in darkness. Up close, the intruder is larger than I expected. All that means is that he will fall harder.

There is no pause. The bolt cutters are swung with indiscriminate force. They pass through the figure as though they were made of smoke. Black traces follow the trajectory of the weapon. My momentum carries me forward and I crash into the dresser located under the window. Model toys and folded clothes fall to the ground around me.

Stunned, I look back. The figure remains. The void within the hood stares down at me like the barrel of a gun. In the second it takes me to get to my feet I notice that an unsteady line of crimson footprints pass through where the intruder stands. Gritting my teeth, the bolt cutters are raised and brought down again. There is no contact. Trails of black smoke chase the improvised weapon into the shelving units. Framed photos crash to the ground. I remain on my feet and swing the bolt cutters around as though shooting for a home run. I watch them pass through the raised hood and bury themselves into the cupboard. Yanking the weapon out pulls the unit over. It topples onto me like a breaking wave. Adrenaline-fuelled muscles cast it aside and it crashes to the ground, another victim of my spree.

Anger forces me to continue. The weapon collides with everything in the room save the intended target. My vision descends into a watery blur. My throat burns. The grip on the rubber handle begins to loosen, friction giving way to the building sweat of my palms.

Letting out a defeated cry, I swing for the last time. The bolt cutters leave my hands and sail through the window. The shattering of glass is deafening. Worse than any squeal of an old swing.

With hands pressed against my temples, I fall back against the wall and slide down onto the toys and pictures that used to be neatly lined up across the shelves.

Tears begin to flow. A saltiness coats my lips. I'm at the mercy of my tormentor, yet he is absent from the triumph. I am alone, as I am destined to be, with the consequences of my impulsive, rage-filled actions for unwanted company.

It hurts to look upon the chaos I've created. I lower my gaze and see a photo frame resting at my side. The glass is cracked but the image is still visible. It is of Patrick playing on his favourite swing, beaming with joy. Janie is in the background, pushing him back and forth, sharing in the captured moment of happiness. I remember taking the photo. I remember that we printed it out and framed it that afternoon. I remember that it was the last day we spent together.

The frame is squeezed within my hands. The wooden frame splinters in resistance then fractures in two, taking the cherished memory with it. It is hurled across the room and added to the carnage. There are now few things left in Patrick's bedroom that have not suffered from the outburst. Up until a few months ago, there was just one defenceless child.

Geisha

(First published on The Other Stories podcast, June 2018)

The black taxi came to an abrupt stop; barely pulling in from the congested road. The scruffy driver spun round in his seat and faced Katrina. Through stained teeth he explained something in a language she couldn't comprehend. With a blank expression, she shrugged her shoulders in response. The driver nodded and walked his fingers across his palm, indicating that she was walking from here.

A broad grin broke across her freckled face and curling a loose lock of auburn hair behind her ear, she dug around in her bag for the fare. Climbing out of the taxi, the full sensory onslaught of Kyoto smothered her. A cacophony of car horns, chatter and sirens assaulted her ears. Undecipherable patterns covered street signs and shop windows. Vehicles clogged the roads and commuters cluttered the wide pavements. She felt as though she had been shrunk down and dropped into an ant's nest.

She began walking down the alley that the taxi driver had pointed to, and it only took a few steps before the change of scenery made it feel as if she had travelled back in time. The buildings morphed from concrete skyscrapers to narrow, two storey refuges. Each one of the ancient, wooden buildings had a balcony that overlooked the paved road that she now walked. The rushing city folk turned into meandering tourists, and red, bulbous lanterns replaced neon lamp posts.

"This must be Gion," she said to herself, and dug out a map in an attempt to make sense of the cryptic street signs that littered the ancient district.

The technology magazine Katrina worked for had received an invite to preview an exciting new product from Sy-Tech—a controversial robotics and AI developer that had been rumoured to implement somewhat unethical practices when it came to R&D. Usually, the young journalist would have passed—she'd seen enough clunky and dull mechanoids masquerading as humans in her short career. But the company's reputation offered the prospect of breaking a story that could propel her into the journalistic big leagues.

She checked her watch for the hundredth time as she negotiated the labyrinth of alleyways lined with pink cherry blossoms and stores selling Japanese trinkets. With only a few minutes to spare, she arrived at her destination. The ageing building looked the same as the hundreds she had passed, save a sign on the front that read 'SY-TECH' in bold white letters. She frowned, expecting something a little more grandiose for a world-leading tech firm. Looking up and down the street and seeing no other better options, she shrugged and pushed the weighty entrance door open.

The simple, well-lit room was bare—as if the owners had sold all of their possessions to pay the electricity bill—save for a single figure stood in the centre, staring at the chipped slats that made up the floor. The person wore a blue robe adorned with floral patterns that climbed up from the hem to the collar and then spread down the arms. A thick head of black hair, darker than night itself, was tied into bunches.

The mysterious figure looked up, revealing a smooth, porcelain-white face. Only the bare minimum of features was visible. Thin black lines hinted at where the eyes, nostrils and eyebrows were, with a small triangle of bright red lipstick the only clue that the figure was female and had a mouth. The figure blinked several times, acknowledging Katrina's presence.

"Er, hello," Katrina attempted. "Konnichiwa."

The woman tilted her head to the side. "Katrina, welcome." Her voice was monotone, lacking any familiarity. "This way, please." She gestured towards a set of wooden doors that promptly slid apart to reveal an elevator.

Katrina hesitated, considering the strange woman for a moment. She glanced at the elevator, and then back at the mysterious receptionist. Raising her hand to say something, she caught herself and instead approached the elevator and stepped in.

The doors closed just as Katrina turned around, allowing only a brief glimpse of the ghostly woman who continued to stare at her with cold eyes. A shiver rippled down her spine as the elevator began its descent.

The doors parted and Katrina's jaw dropped at the sight of an almost futuristic world. Glass walls and marble floors created a grand entrance lobby that extended high above her. A large screen on the wall played what appeared to be a promotional video, showing clips of scientists in labs and robotic arms building machinery and microchips.

A formally dressed man in a dark suit greeted a stunned Katrina with a broad smile. His dark hair was shiny and combed tightly into a side parting. He had a fine complexion as if he had applied a thick layer of makeup.

"Good morning, Katrina," the man said with an American accent. "I'm Simon, pleased to meet you."

Katrina relaxed and stepped forward with her arm extended, inviting a handshake.

The man's posture stiffened. He dropped his hands to his side and bowed. Katrina mentally cursed herself, retracting her open palm in the process. She imitated the same bowing gesture; still struggling to adjust to this foreign land and its customs.

They both straightened and faced each other. The welcoming smile remained on the man's flawless face. "You managed to find us then."

"Yes, just about."

"We like to keep a low profile around here." Simon turned and began leading Katrina to one of the rooms. "You're just in time; the presentation is about to begin."

"Is that your receptionist upstairs?"

"Ah, yes. I hope she was on her best behaviour. We've had some... issues with that one."

Katrina frowned. "Issues?"

Simon ignored the question. "Here we are."

They stepped into a meeting room full of journalists chatting amongst themselves. They faced a small stage at the far end of the room that was covered by a thick, red curtain.

"Please take a seat," Simon instructed. He left Katrina and joined two other men waiting on the stage. She studied the three of them, intrigued as to how similar they all looked with identical hairstyles, posture and suits. Shaking the xenophobic observation away, she pulled out her Dictaphone and notepad.

"Ladies and gentlemen," one of the other men began, addressing the crowd in the same American accent. "My name is Stuart. Thank you all for coming. As you are all aware, Sy-Tech has an exciting new development that we are pleased to unveil to you today. So without further ado, please put your hands together for our new line of geishas."

To the sound of applause, the curtain was raised to reveal five women all identical to the receptionist that had greeted Katrina upstairs. They stood motionless, staring into the distance.

"Geishas, please say hello."

The five geishas blinked in unison, and then raised a hand, waving and smiling to the crowd. Their movements were even and natural, without any hint of the motors and gears that lay within.

Stuart continued with his presentation. "As you can see, we have made many developments in the world of robotics and AI. Based on the traditional female entertainers, each geisha is programmed to meet all of your home entertainment needs. Whether it's cooking, cleaning, dancing or even light conversation."

A murmur spread through the room as the crowd scribbled down notes and took photos.

"Observe. Geishas, fan dance," Stuart requested.

In unison, the geishas pulled out fans from within their robes and began to bob and move around the stage in a perfectly choreographed sequence. Their movements were exact, as if they were a reflection of a single lead performer.

When the dance came to an end, Stuart continued. "But of course, any robot can dance. But how many can cook?" A table full of utensils and ingredients was rolled onto the stage. "Who would like some sushi?"

From within the audience, a hand shot up into the air.

Stuart beamed, revealing a mouth of perfectly square teeth. "Excellent. Some tempura anyone?"

Several more eager journalists raised their hands.

"Geishas, please prepare some sushi and tempura for our guests."

The geishas blinked into life and set to work. They operated as a team of chefs, moving between each other and selecting and preparing various ingredients.

Katrina watched from the front row, her interest piqued. These robots were decades ahead of anything she had ever witnessed. Their actions were so real and convincing. She scrutinised the geisha on the far end of the lineup as she cut into a chunk of bright red tuna. The knife sliced through the flesh with ease. The geisha suddenly winced, causing creases to spread across her pale, empty face. A trickle of red began to seep from her finger.

Stuart saw it too and quickly spoke up, his voice louder and more authoritative than before. "As you can see, we have gone to great lengths to create the most realistic androids possible." He turned to face the mechanoids. "Thank you, geishas."

The robots froze at this command, left to gaze into the distance as if their power cords had been yanked from the sockets.

Stuart turned back to the audience. "Unfortunately, there are still a few bugs in the system. We may have to reset that one." Katrina was certain she saw the eyes of the wounded geisha widen at the comment. "Now on with the tour."

Stuart led the group out of the presentation room and back into the entrance lobby. The promotional video was still playing, appearing to show a geisha in a suburban home; a smiling husband, wife and son were all sat around a dining table as the robotic servant cooked dinner. The tour group passed through a set of large double doors and walked down a glass-walled corridor, allowing them to observe a busy workshop in action. Mechanical arms swung left and right. Sparks danced into the air and drill bits spun as a procession of contraptions were ferried along the production line. At each consecutive station, the collection of robotic parts became more and more human-like.

Katrina trailed along at the back, barely hearing Stuart's spiel over the sound of the workshop. They entered a large room full of perspex boxes containing enlarged electrical boards and microchips. As the reporters gathered around one of the displays, captivated by its contents, Katrina noticed a door with 'Restricted Access' written across it in bold letters. She surveyed the room—this could be the opportunity she needed to make her story stand out from the crowd. After all, it's easier to get forgiveness than permission.

Holding a sharp inhale, she slipped through the door into a darkened room. She fumbled around for a light switch but found none. With a sigh, she went to leave when a murmur caught her attention. It sounded like a muffled gag. Her eyes began to adjust to the lack of light, allowing shapes within the room to become more defined. Soon a row of white faces began to emerge like summoned apparitions.

Lines of geishas stood before her, all emitting stifled cries. With a ruffled brow, she moved in closer and placed her ear against the chest of one of the geishas. She felt it rise and fall, and could hear the faint sound of a rhythmical thudding within. Then somewhere in the distance, as if trapped down a deep well, she thought she heard someone cry, "Help me."

Surgical white light filled the room as lamps along the ceiling burst into life. Katrina squinted, holding up her hand to shield her eyes.

"I see you've found our collection of geishas." One of the men from the presentation – she couldn't tell which one – was stood behind her, his hands clasped at his waist. His eyes were fixated on her, his mouth showing the smallest of grins.

"Simon. I mean, Stuart," Katrina stammered, trying to regain some composure. "Where did you—doesn't matter. What are these... things?"

"Why, these are our new line of geishas."

Katrina waved a shaking hand at the rows of androids lined up like Terracotta Warriors. "I heard a call for help... and... and a heartbeat."

The man shook his head like a disappointed parent. "Oh, that is a shame."

"What?" Katrina took a step back. "What have you done?" Her voice was trembling as the pieces started to fall into place.

"Did you not hear during the presentation?" The man's pupils began to glow red; his face started to resemble an old ventriloquist dummy. "We've made many advances in the world of robotics and AI."

He moved towards her, his mouth now a gaping, sick smile that revealed a set of whirring gears and cogs within.

The Wind Chimes

(First published in 'Midnight Echo 14', November 2019)

It was not a soothing sound. If I had to describe it, I would say it was almost morbid, and would not be out of place at a funeral.

The gentle knocking of wind chimes used to remind me of peace and tranquillity. Of dream catchers and braided pendants. Of surfing trips and intimate, grassroots festivals.

But not these, these were different.

A dry gust of wind, warmed by the heat of the surrounding desert, flows over the porch and invigorates the macabre sound once again.

I lean back on the swing chair. It lets out a long creak. My eyes narrow as I consider the decoration. The wood is smooth and pale. At each end is a bulbous knot that bursts forth like a cancerous growth. The thought sends a shiver through my tired body.

The faint tinkle of ice cubes on glass brings my attention to the front door of this decrepit house. It promptly swings open and a stained tumbler full of cloudy water appears. It is carried by Carrie-Anne. She flashes a black-toothed grin at me and hands me the glass. Tears of condensation are already trickling down the side of it.

"Thank you," I mutter, trying my best to avoid eye contact. I looked upon her cloudy eyes just once, when she picked me up, and I'd been avoiding them ever since. The woman is as ragged as the building she calls home. Her grey hair streaks in all directions like the branches of some long-dead tree, and her hands are covered in sores; skin peels from them like the flaking paint of the swing door. Those hands touched the same glass I'm expected to drink from.

"Lucky I was passing by when I was," Carrie-Anne says. "Not many people out this way."

I nod and stare out at the desolate scrubland, wondering if luck is relative.

My host motions towards the untouched glass. "You must be thirsty?"

The cloudiness of the liquid reminds me of her distant eyes.

"Don't mind the colour," Carrie-Anne says. "The water's a little off out here. Give it a min, it'll settle."

My throat is dry and my stomach aches, but for the moment I'd rather endure the thirst. There are more pressing matters at hand. "Is it just you out here, on your own?"

"Usually," Carrie-Anne replies.

I can't think of anything else to say. An empty silence fills the void until the wind chime sways into life.

I glance up and notice its smaller details. Misshapen nuggets, the size of molars, are strung together like a dirty pearl necklace. "Interesting decoration."

"I made it," Carrie-Anne says, looking pleased with herself.

"What wood is that?" I ask.

That horrid smile returns. "You must be thirsty."

Tipua

It's out there, waiting. I'm certain of it. One of those trees, the one that is covered in leaves that are too perfect and has branches that are too angular, doesn't move like the others. It pretends to sway from side to side with the wind, but I can tell.

If I try to remember how this all started, then it would be within the dark, creaking depths of that ship. I hated that ship; the endless chores, the thick humid air, never being more than five metres from another crewmate. We'd been at sea for months—or was it years?—navigating the South Pacific. For what, I might ask? So King George can add another spice to his decadent banquets? So the captain can plant the Union Jack into another far-flung rock that no one cares about?

My good friend Robert and I were ordered to tally supplies. A job few volunteered for. It's as black as a kraken's eye down there. Huddled in that claustrophobic space, with barrels stacked high above us and our rough bearded faces illuminated by flickering candlelight, we checked and counted. I had gone only a few paces from Robert when an almighty crash startled me. The commotion caused the candle to slip from my grasp and be extinguished on the mouldy, damp floor.

To be in absolute darkness is an unsettling experience. Without the power of sight, the other senses heighten. Suddenly you can taste the salt on your tongue, feel the stale air on your skin, and smell the sharp tang of alcohol stored in the casks of rum. But it's your hearing that sharpens the most. The creaking of the ship's timber hull cracks like lightning. The dripping of water becomes a high-pitched plip that makes you wince.

However, it was Robert's cry for help that cut through all of these senses. I could feel every muscle that was being crushed and discern the breath leaving his lungs with each shallow gasp. Navigating by my only means necessary, I ran my calloused hands along the wooden casks as I searched for my trapped friend. His voice echoed around the hold, confusing and disorienting me. Lost in the dark, I stumbled over something fleshy that let out a muffled cry. Regaining my balance, I fumbled in the void to find Robert pinned under several barrels. With all my might I shoved them off him, hearing them thud and roll around on the galley floor.

We could hear voices and footsteps above us and soon the hold began to fill with crew members and precious light. Lifting Robert under the arms, we dragged him out as best we could. It was later that night, when I was sat by Robert's side in the infirmary, that we decided to free ourselves of this ship, of this life. At the next landing we would make our escape. Desertion carries a heavy penalty, but only if you're caught.

It was a week or so later that a cry from the crow's nest told of land on the horizon—some place called New Zealand. I'd heard many tales of its natural beauty and fierce Maori inhabitants; warriors who tower over the average man with tattooed faces, bulging eyes and lizard-like tongues.

The following day, with loaded rifles on our laps, a small group of us rowed ashore. At the bow of the boat was Rua—a dark-skinned, friendly islander that had joined us at a previous stop. The missionaries had got to him a few years ago and for all their faults, had taught him and his tribe the language of the civilised world. The captain had allowed him to join us, thinking that his language skills may prove useful.

A line of warriors awaited our arrival, and before our vessel had even ground to a halt on the golden sand, Rua had jumped out. With his hands splayed in front of him, he slowly approached while speaking in some incomprehensible dialect.

The rest of us remained on the boat, our fingers tensed around rifle triggers, staring intently at the exchange.

On the beach, stern faces turned to broad smiles, and within minutes we were welcomed onto their land. Up close, the natives were far more welcoming than the stories had made out. While we greeted each other I noticed that a greenstone was worn around many of their necks. The smooth rock was a colour and composition of which I'd never seen before—it was as if a piece of the forest had been compressed into a beautifully curved pendant. My eyes widened at the thought of how much a precious stone like that would be worth back in the civilised world.

That evening, sat around a raging bonfire, the hospitable locals entertained us with exotic foods, dancing, and stories that Rua attempted to translate for us.

There were huge giants that stepped from mountain to mountain and drank rivers and lakes dry.

Then there were the tiny, pale-skinned fairies known as pakepakeha that could be seen floating down rivers laughing and singing.

And finally, there was the tipua—a shape shifting being that dwelled within the dense forests and could take any form it desired. It guarded the pounamu - the greenstones I'd noticed earlier - only allowing them to be taken if they were to be gifted to a loved one.

The crew members and I smiled along politely; it wasn't the first time we'd heard such nonsense from simple natives. They probably thought the world was flat too.

The following morning Robert and I approached some locals and attempted to coax them into gifting their stones to us. None of them could be swayed, with many muttering something about tipua. So instead we gathered together our possessions so we could trade. I had a tarnished snuff box and a bronze pocket watch. Robert's contribution was less impressive, with a stained handkerchief and a pair of tattered shoes. With a mischievous grin, he disappeared for several minutes and returned with a selection of polished musket balls.

However, it was not possible to find one native that would part with their pendant, regardless of how much shiny metal we offered.

Undeterred, we tried a different approach, and with the help of Rua, managed to convince one of the local boys to show us where the stones lay. All it took was a handful of lead balls - the boy's eyes lighting up at the sight of them - saving me from having to relinquish my timepiece.

Soon Robert and I were engulfed by vegetation as we followed the boy deeper and deeper into the forest. Our guide didn't seem to follow a path, but instead navigated via strewn boulders and fallen trees that littered the endless greens and browns that surrounded us.

We followed him blindly for hours until eventually arriving at a secluded waterfall. The tumbling water splashed into a shallow pool before continuing on its journey. At first we thought he'd stopped to take a drink, but as he bent down he picked something up and showed it to us. Intrigued, we moved in for a closer look; nestled in the palm of his hand was a greenstone. I reached out to take it but the boy snatched his hand back. We locked eyes and he cautioned something in his mother-tongue, his voice now serious and grave. That word tipua was uttered again.

Robert and I nodded in understanding. We then looked at each other and exchanged the smallest of smiles. The boy considered us for a moment, then glanced up at the sky. It was beginning to darken. He shrugged his shoulders and lay down next to the river, content to sleep on the rough ground until the sun rose for another day. Without saying a word, we waited until the boy's breathing deepened and slowed. We then began filling our pockets.

I slept well that night, exhausted from the hike, but also comforted by what riches awaited once we arrived back home. I fantasised over the trading company I would set up, the riches I could lavish upon my mistresses, my new life in the upper echelons of society.

The soothing thoughts were rudely shaken away by the boy as he tried to wake me. It was morning, and he was pulling at my sleeve, wanting us to leave right away. The youngster seemed agitated. He struggled to focus on me, his attention constantly drawn to the surrounding trees.

"All right, all right," I muttered, getting to my feet. Unbeknownst to me, several greenstones had slipped from my pocket while I slept.

The boy gasped at the sight of them. Before I could attempt to explain he broke into a run, swallowed up by the forest in seconds.

I looked over at Robert, who just shrugged. "Guess we're finding our own way out of here." He flicked a pilfered greenstone into the air as if it was a coin while sporting that same mischievous grin as before. It didn't take long before it was wiped from his face.

With no other bearings to work from, we headed in the direction the boy fled, doing our best to locate his footprints and hopefully follow them back to the coast.

It was only when we slowed to check which way to go that I noticed the silence.

"You hear that?" I asked.

"Hear what?" Robert replied.

"Exactly." During our walk the previous day the canopy and undergrowth had been teeming with birds, their calls filling the woodland. But now, nothing. Just the footsteps and heavy breathing of two lost foreigners. "This isn't right," I cautioned. "Something isn't right."

The forest felt different. The tree bark was rougher, the greens more vivid, the earth under our feet more compact. And there was something always there, just in my peripheral vision. A subtle movement that I was unable to identify. A shadow almost, that was continually at my side.

Robert turned to face me. His complexion was paler than before; his eyes more distant. "You think that kid is spying on us?"

I just nodded in reply.

Robert continued, "I just get this feeling that we're being watched, you know?"

The same thought had crossed my mind not long after we left the waterfall. With my hands in my pockets, I turned over the stash of greenstones between my fingers, feeling the smooth surface against my clammy skin. For a moment I wondered what we had gotten ourselves into.

The worrying thought was interrupted by a rustling and Robert suddenly being dragged into the undergrowth. It was as if the trees had burst into life, freeing themselves from their deep roots and rigid stances, and enveloped Robert. The last thing I saw was a pair of kicking boots being dragged from sight.

I tore off in the opposite direction, forcing my way through branches and vines that gripped and clung at my clothes. I leapt over roots that grasped my feet, and I dodged boulders that seemed to block my way.

And in that frantic blur of panic-filled escape the shadow was always there. It moved with me. Almost anticipating my every move.

I drove on, forcing one foot in front of the other. My muscles burned, screaming out for me to stop. My lungs inflated and deflated like bellows as I tried to breathe in the thick humid air. Just as I felt I could go on no longer, the trees parted to reveal a cave, the only place this shadow couldn't follow me.

I stumbled towards it, falling onto my hands and knees, and scurried into its gloomy interior. It was not deep, perhaps only a few metres, but the sanctuary was dark enough to offer protection from that which stalked me.

And it's here that I now sit, curled up at the back of this cold and damp place. The dank air smells of sweat. The sound of trees shaking in the wind scrapes against my eardrums. The stolen treasure that fills my pockets feels like broken glass against my skin.

I wait from it in here. And it waits for me out there. We've been at this standoff for hours now. It'll be dark soon. I've outwitted this being, this tipua. Maybe I'll be able to make it to the coast before sunrise and flee to the safety of the ship. I just need to hold on for a few more... wait! I can hear something. No! Someone. It's distant, but it sounds like... my God, it's Robert. He's calling out to me. He's alive. He needs my help.

I shuffle to the front of the cave. I hesitate, just for a moment, but his desperate cries overcome any doubt.

I climb out and feel the warm, comforting daylight on my skin. A relieved smile comes across my face. "I'm coming, my friend. I'm coming."

Fingerprints

A shaky voice crackles over the police radio, full of muddled words and long pauses. Janus Evergreen takes his hand off the steering wheel and reaches over to turn up the volume. He usually would have ignored it. He and Patterson are heading back to the station. It's been a long enough day as it is—he's already lied twice to his wife about what time he would be home. But there is something about the officer's voice that catches his attention.

After another extended pause, the voice on the radio requests backup. Janus glances over at Patterson. She greets him with an expectant stare. Strands of brown hair have escaped her tight ponytail; her blemished skin is beginning to show through her thinning makeup. Without a word, she rolls her eyes and leans back into the passenger seat.

Janus reaches for the intercom. "This is detectives Evergreen and Patterson responding. En route. ETA six minutes."

Eight minutes later, Janus and Patterson turn onto a leafy, tree-lined street. The flashing red and blue lights of the awaiting patrol vehicle illuminate the warm night.

Two officers are parked outside one of the many obscenely large properties that make up the neighbourhood. They both lean on the hood of their vehicle. The taller of the two men draws heavily on a cigarette. The other stouter man has his hat pulled down low, almost covering his eyes. Rolling up onto the curb, Janus can't remember the last time he saw an officer of the law smoking. He gave up years ago, but a bent and twisted pack of Marlboros remains in the glove box all the same. The last time the cigarettes were needed was the orphanage case. He shudders at the memory and thinks of those little white nicotine sticks now, and whether he'll need one tonight.

The officers offer little concerning what awaits the detectives inside the house. They appear distracted, their faces pale and drawn. The lips of the smoker barely move as he speaks. "You'll need to see for yourself." The cigarette is drawn down to the filter. It's flicked away without regard and another instantly takes its place. The one who wears the hat simply shakes his head and stares off into the distance.

Janus exchanges a look with Patterson. She wearily shrugs but says nothing. Janus nods in understanding. Patterson stays with the officers—she may be able to coax some useful information out of them. Janus goes to search the property.

He gazes upon the house with its ornate archway, perfect hanging baskets and manicured lawn. The heavy front door, complete with brass knocker, hangs open. Before Janus is over the threshold he can see the mess in the narrow hallway. Picture frames and artworks lie strewn across the carpet. The scattered glass pieces reflect the flashing lights from the patrol car outside, turning the floor into a strobing mosaic.

Moving through the hallway, taking care not to disturb the disorder underfoot, Janus notices that many of the photos are covered in fingerprints. He reaches inside his jacket and pulls out a pair of surgical gloves. Slipping his hands into the thin latex that stretches against his skin, he picks up one of the frames: the perfect family portrait, taken on a white beach with a calm turquoise ocean in the background, is defaced with two elongated crimson swirls. He is about to place it down when a detail catches his eye. The frame is held up to the light. He tilts it back and forth, unsatisfied with what he is seeing. Eventually, he rubs his thumb across the corner of one of the fingerprints. The print goes undisturbed. He tries again, this time sliding his thumb right across the glass. Both prints remain. Janus frowns at the realisation that the prints are on the inside. The photo is slowly returned to the ground as he attempts to process this detail.

The buzzing of his mobile phone derails his train of thought. Reaching into his pocket, the device is pulled out. He expects it to be Patterson, but it is his wife calling. Her smiling image fills the screen. She'll want to know when to expect him home? Will he still want dinner? How was his day? After a moment of hesitation, Janus cancels the call and returns the phone. He will deal with the repercussions later.

An artwork rests against the foot of the wall—one of those splatter paint jobs he could never afford. Bloody handprints are smeared across the glass. Janus runs a finger through them. Again, the prints appear to be on the inside.

Droplets of sweat gather across Janus's brow. He tells himself it's the humid night air. He looks through the entranceway and sees Patterson talking with the officers. It appears as though she is counselling two widowers. He also sees his vehicle. The image of the stashed cigarettes in the glove box flashes across his mind.

Swallowing hard, Janus moves further into the house. He passes a spacious living room. A glass coffee table has been reduced to a million tiny pieces; a bar stool remains upturned in what is left of it. The screen of the mounted television is now a silver spider web of cracks. Something seeps from the fractures. Red spots multiply on the cream carpet below. He chooses not to enter—forensics can deal with them.

The kitchen is visible at the end of the hallway. It seems to have been spared the destruction laid upon the other rooms. It is as immaculate as the front of the house. Glistening pots and pans hang above clear work surfaces. The black tiled floor appears unused, as if installed moments before he arrived. Everything is in its place, save for one detail.

In the centre of the kitchen table is an opened cardboard box. Brown stuffing paper lies on either side. Frowning, Janus approaches. He peers inside. A black sphere, the size of a billiard ball, sits innocently within the package. The smooth surface gives the impression that it is made of marble or glass.

Janus tilts his head to better read the mailing slip printed on the box. It merely states 'To the occupant', followed by the property's address. He stares down at the object in the package, finding himself entranced by its perfect form. On closer inspection it appears to be filled with a mist or fog that floats within the sphere.

His mobile phone rings again. Janus reaches for it, cursing at the interruption. The grinning image of his wife greets him. The call is promptly cancelled. The phone is stuffed back into his pocket.

He scoops up the ball. It fits neatly within his palm and is heavier than expected. The curved surface is unblemished. The mist contained within, swirls. The flawless sphere is held up inches from his face. Something begins to emerge from the haze. Janus squints, struggling to make it out in the gloom of the kitchen light.

The thing morphs into a face, with features becoming more defined as they break free from the foggy shroud. Janus's eyes widen as the features merge with those of the detective peering into the black ball. A curved reflection stares back at him with panicked eyes. A silent scream is emitted from a gaping mouth.

A fearful gasp escapes Janus's lungs. The sphere is dropped. It lands on the wooden table without a sound. It does not bounce. It does not roll. It remains perfectly still. The mist within, reclaims Janus's distressed reflection.

Janus scans the kitchen, hoping that this is all some elaborate prank: that his colleagues will leap out and shout 'surprise!'; that streamers will fall from the ceiling and corks will fly from champagne bottles. But he's not that lucky.

His sights fall back on the ball. A shiver tingles down his spine. There are other rooms to check, but they can wait. He needs to be free of this place and outside in the warm air and the company of Patterson.

Janus steps back into the neon hallway that continues to strobe red and blue. He notices that the door opposite the kitchen is ajar.

He pauses, glancing between the beckoning normality of outside and the stifling confusion within. He licks his lips, tasting the saltiness of the accumulating sweat, and finds that he is nudging the door open before he can stop himself. It silently swings on its hinges to reveal a toilet, washbasin and laminate flooring streaked with two parallel lines of thick blood. Janus blinks sweat from his eyes as he traces the horrid stains to the base of a shattered full-length mirror. Hundreds of shimmering pieces are scattered throughout the room, as though something had burst free of the reflective surface.

It is just possible to make out footprints going from what remains of the mirror to the wall opposite. A mobile phone lies on the ground, where the streaks begin. Something was dragged across the floor. Janus corrects himself—someone was dragged across the floor. But where are they now?

Janus lets out a long breath. His bulky frame deflates a little. He's seen enough and wants out. He needs some air. He needs a smoke. His hurried footfalls clumsily stomp through the shattered mess in the hallway. There will be angry words from forensics later; he doesn't care.

The warm night greets him. It feels like a safety blanket. As his muscles relax the phone buzzes again. Without thinking he pulls it out. He has no intention of answering, but the prospect of seeing the photo of his loving wife is comforting. His thumb is already over the cancel button when he looks at the screen. His world shifts, almost knocking him off his feet. It is not the picture of his wife that greets him. Instead, it is the same warped face that is trapped inside the black sphere. Janus holds up the phone that shakes within his grasp. They meet each other's stare, and then a filthy hand reaches out, the palm pressing up against the inside of the screen.

Janus screams. The phone clatters on the concrete path. Specks of blood fly out as though the device is wounded.

The two officers look up.

Patterson calls out, asking if he is okay.

Janus stumbles forward, waving his arm dismissively. His vehicle is just there. He needs a minute alone. He needs to think. He really needs that smoke.

The car door slams behind him as he falls into the driver's seat. The doors are locked. He is faintly aware of the urgent, dull tones of Patterson shouting at the window. The glove box is popped open. Papers and manuals are torn out, falling across the passenger seat and foot well. The crumpled pack of Marlboros is snatched at. The few cigarettes that remain are emptied into trembling hands. Janus clamps one between his lips. The lighter takes several flicks of the flint to spark a flame. He sucks deeply. Soothing nicotine fills his lungs. He rocks back and forth in the driver's seat, failing to push the events of the last few minutes from his mind.

Patterson taps on the window. It is ignored. Eventually, she gives up and says something about going to look inside for herself.

Janus's body stiffens. He goes to warn her but before he can, he catches sight of a figure in the rear view mirror. Someone shares the car with him. It's the same person from inside the black ball, from inside the mobile phone. Instinctively he reaches for his holstered revolver and snaps around to confront the intruder. But the rear seats are empty.

Janus lets out a relieved sigh. Smoke catches in his throat. He coughs, and then swivels back around, just in time to be showered in glass as a pair of ragged hands bursts from the rear view mirror.

A Grave Mistake

I've always loved cemeteries. I couldn't tell you how many I've visited over the years, how many miles I've covered strolling through rows of headstones, how many hours I've whiled away sat on benches. The scent of freshly-laid flowers in the air, the sensation of polished granite at my fingertips, the hushed exchanges of other visitors. The experience really is quite unique. Of course, I have my favourites.

There's the La Recoleta in Buenos Aires that consists of an impressive and varied array of mausoleums and memorials. They're so tall and packed together so tightly that it is like walking down a macabre high street.

Then there is the Old Jewish Cemetery in Prague. The headstones are practically piled up on top of each other, fighting for space to mark the equally crowded graves below.

Greenwood Cemetery in New York is another favourite, with its vast open spaces and greenery. Such a lovely area to wander and gather your thoughts while escaping the bustle of the city.

But I have to admit, there is a particular one that I find myself returning to again and again—Lowestoft Cemetery. I imagine you may not have heard of it. Situated on the east coast of England in the charming county of Suffolk, at a glance it may not appear special or particularly interesting. The graves span outwards from the small church in orderly rows. Proud oak trees coat the ground in brown leaves during autumn. The grass is kept trimmed; gravel paths crunch under the footsteps of mourners. The church bell sounds twice daily and never fails to shock the surrounding birds into flight. It's all very modest and quaint.

There are probably two reasons why I visit here so often. The first is the age of this place. It's one of the oldest cemeteries in Great Britain. I do love my history, and there's almost a thousand years of it here. It shouldn't come as much of a surprise looking at the state of some of the headstones. Time has eroded the engravings from many of the oldest ones, reducing them to nothing more than chunks of concrete that lean at a precarious angle. I shouldn't be so critical; they've outlasted the church. The crooked spire, slate roof and stained-glass windows have either been replaced or rebuilt several times throughout the centuries. I seldom venture inside. It's difficult to shake the feeling that I'm not welcome. I bet there isn't a single original pew or rafter in there.

But I digress. The other reason for visiting is because they say you can hear the cries of the dead in this place. It's nonsense, of course. Although I have to admit, one of my guilty pleasures is watching visitors and mourners pause as they pass by. With flowers in one hand and tissues in the other, a growing expression of concern spreads across their faces. Sitting on this very bench, peering out from under the brim of my hat, I often get asked, "Did you hear that?" I politely smile and shake my head. Sometimes I notice them shiver as though chilled by a brisk icy wind. Then they're on their way, at a quicker pace than before. If any of these worried individuals took a moment to inspect the headstones at the spot where they heard these so-called cries, they would notice that three of the unassuming, moss-covered headstones have something in common—the date in which the deceased was buried, and the surnames chiselled into six hundred-year-old granite.

Their story begins in the year thirteen-forty-seven when the Victorm docked into the Sicilian port of Messina. Many of the crew were already dead, their withered and rotting corpses strewn throughout the ship. The survivors lacked the strength to cast their fellow sailors over the side, for their own frail bodies were riddled with plague. The Black Death had arrived in Europe.

It spread at a speed the Four Horsemen would be proud of, indiscriminately striking down anyone in its path. Black buboes would expand like cancerous growths in the neck, groin and armpits. After causing continuous bouts of shivering, vomiting and diarrhoea, the final and inevitable last step was death.

Cemeteries were overrun, leading to a variety of solutions for dealing with the deceased that piled up in the streets. Mass graves were dug to accommodate the thousands of dead. In Siena, the bodies were thrown into the foundation pits of the old city walls. Piles of jumbled skeletons remain there to this day. Pope Clement the Sixth consecrated the entire Rhone River so that bodies could be dumped into the waters and washed away by the current.

All the while, physicians struggled to find a cure. Some recommended blood-letting and rubbing chopped up snake and pigeon into the buboes. Others championed the consumption of arsenic and mercury. Thinking positive thoughts and huddling up to raging fires were other ineffective treatments.

Chaos swept across Europe but had yet to arrive onto the shores of Great Britain. The only thing that travelled faster than the plague was word of its devastation. The grim facts were brought to the sleepy English village of Lowestoft by Samuel Burton, a ruthless entrepreneur who broke free of feudal society and travelled throughout mainland Europe. Samuel was well-turned-out and carried himself with an air of authority. In contrast, his three younger brothers - David, Matthew and Thomas - were hunched and downtrodden from a life working on the lands of nobility.

Always one to see an opportunity in any situation, no matter how dire, Samuel returned home with a business proposition for his brothers. With landowners and bloodlines being wiped out, there were significant gains to be made if they played their cards right. There was one small issue of course; they needed to survive the plague. It was then that the brothers came to learn that Samuel didn't just bring back news from the continent, but also the dark ways of the occult—the key to their fortune.

And so it was, on a still night with the full moon hanging high in the sky, the four Burton brothers gathered within a dilapidated barn on the village outskirts. The air thick with the stench of farm animals, manure and blood, they swayed and chanted around a crimson pentagram crudely drawn in the dirt. Their cloaked shadows shifted and moved in the candlelight. Flies swarmed and rats scurried in the dark corner of the stable where the discarded body of a young girl lay. A ritual detail that Samuel had kept to himself and arranged before the arrival of his siblings—there was, after all, no need to give them a reason to back out.

All the sacrifice, pomp and ceremony worked as desired. Thomas was first to notice, while glancing over at his brothers in the hope that they shared his reservations regarding the ritual. He initially thought that the shifting light was playing tricks on him. But then the bony arch of an elbow came into view, a hand pressing into the ground. Then another. A head and torso peeled themselves from the dirt floor. Several heinous seconds later, the limp body of the butchered girl emerged from the shadows. Her pale skin glistened in the light. Her once-floral dress that now hung from her skinny frame was stained beyond recognition. Lifeless arms hung at her side. Thin, bent legs moved with an unnatural gait, as though unfamiliar with the concept of walking. Long matted hair hid her face, but the tilted angle of her head exhibited a deep slash across her neck. Blood trickled from the wound that coloured her footprints.

Thomas's gasp alerted the others. The chanting and swaying ceased. The brothers watched in stunned horror as the resurrected girl shuffled to the centre of the pentagram. There she remained, rocking ever so slightly from side to side.

A gargled female voice finally shattered the silence. "You seek immortality?"

The candles burned a little brighter, holding back darkness that felt colder and denser than before.

Samuel spoke, his trembling voice betraying an attempt at confidence. "Dark Lord, we wish to be immune from this plague. Grant us that one wish, I beg of you."

The girl continued to sway as she spoke, the shifting light exaggerating and warping her movement. "I deal only with the devoted."

Samuel glared at his brothers. Each one of them cowered before this manifestation of evil, their eyes wide with fear. There was no admiration for this supreme being. Sensing that the opportunity was slipping away, Samuel threw himself to his knees in desperation. "I promise you we are all your loyal servants."

"Very well. You must prove your devotion. To walk this earth for eternity, you must first walk through the gates of hell."

Not a second later, the girl collapsed—the use of her body no longer required. The candles returned to their usual warm glow; the darkness thinned a little.

David, Matthew and Thomas exchanged a look of concern. Terror, or perhaps worry, rooted them to the spot. What had they just witnessed? What had they agreed to? What were they doing here?

However, Samuel did not share their sense of trepidation. He knew what needed to be done.

"No, wait!" David cried before the blade was plunged into his throat.

Samuel barely paused between striking Thomas and lunging at Matthew.

Matthew gasped as the knife sank deep into his chest. The weapon was removed before Matthew could raise his hands to it. He fell backwards, palms covering a bloody cavity, as though in preparation for his burial.

Thomas managed a stifled cry for help as he fled. The thrown blade dug into his back, forcing him to the ground. However, it was enough.

Moments later, Samuel was discovered. Alerted by Thomas's cry, a farmer and his brother came to investigate. After a brief scuffle, Samuel was overcome before he could take his own life. Pinned to the ground, his shouts and protests echoed into the night.

Judge and jury acted swiftly in those days. The damning evidence of Samuel's blood-spattered face, four dead bodies and a pentagram etched into the dirt, amounted to a sentence of burning at the stake. The following evening, as the sun slipped over the horizon, the woodpile was lit. The wind became tainted with ash, burning flesh and the suffering cries of a committed devil worshipper. At the same time, on the other side of the village, three brothers presumed innocent in this terrible business, were boxed up and laid to rest in Lowestoft Cemetery.

Were they right to bargain with Lucifer? Well, within a year the Black Death had ravished the village, claiming ninety per cent of its inhabitants. I'm not a gambling man, but I'd say that those aren't bad odds.

And you may think that the four brothers were cheated; conned out of their side of the deal. And I'd argue that I'm a busy man with many affairs to attend. I granted them what they sought, but I can't be held responsible for the actions of the villagers while the brothers proved their faith down below.

You know, after the sentencing, Samuel was the subject of his own story: the man who burned longer and screamed louder than anyone could remember. They kept the fire burning for three long days. When it was left to burn down, and a quiet whimper could still be heard, the charred body was dismembered and buried in an unmarked grave. Unfortunately, even my powers have their limitations.

As for the three brothers? Well, I knew that they were never committed; that the plan and ritual were all Samuel's doing. But a deal is a deal, and I am a man of my word.

Like the many cemeteries dotted across the globe or the forms I assume while up here, life and death can be many things. It's something I like to ponder in the afternoon sun while watching visitors to Lowestoft

Cemetery pause for the briefest of moments, certain that they heard a distant cry or muffled yell.

When I said it was nonsense that people could hear the cries of the dead, I wasn't entirely lying. They're the cries of three immortal brothers begging to be released from their side of the bargain.

Frozen Bodies and Shallow Graves

The heavy door swings open, creaking on its hinges. Liz steps through, her shoes squelching underfoot. The prospect of being out of wet cycling gear is a comforting thought. The warmth of the hut interior is instantly welcoming—nothing compares to a log fire. However, the feeling of bliss is fleeting. If the fire is lit, then someone else must be at the hut. The place appeared deserted on first impressions; she could see no visible lights. There were no boots or bags in the porch area as she entered.

"Looks like you made it just in time."

The voice startles Liz, despite the soft and welcoming tone. She scans the communal area and sees a silhouette hunched over one of the tables in the corner. Her back straightens. Her mind visualises the multi-tool within her pocket and whether it is possible to position the corkscrew attachment between her fingers as a crude means of self-defence.

The voice speaks again, remaining within the shadows. "My apologies, I didn't mean to give you a fright."

"Are there no lights in here?" Liz asks, taking a step backwards.

"These huts have a lot of luxuries - gas for hot water is a nice touch - but electricity is not one of them."

"Don't you have a torch?" The question flies out as more of an accusation.

The figure stands, arms extended, fingers splayed. "Again, my apologies, I fear we may have got off on the wrong foot. I arrived a while ago. I saw that the weather was turning and lit the fire. And since then I've been enjoying a wee drink while the sun sets."

Liz watches as the darkened figure turns and collects a bottle off the table. They're similar in build; she may even be a little taller. And the weariness of his voice puts him in the sixty to seventy age bracket. She relaxes a little, but her fingers toy with the multi-tool all the same.

He turns to face her again, wine bottle in hand. He moves into the flickering light of the log fire and for the first time Liz gets a good look at him. Judging by the wrinkles and liver spots it appears her initial guess at an age bracket was generous. He'd have had a good decade or two of collecting a pension, not that it appeared to have done him any good. His thinning white hair has been combed over in an attempt to cover his baldness. Dressed all in black, with the only dash of colour being the tartan scarf wrapped around his neck, Liz can't shake the ludicrous thought that he appears like a lost Scottish mime. He holds the bottle out as a peace offering. "Look, can I interest you in a drink? Warm the cockles and all that. Will warn you now that it's got a bit of a kick. Call it my 'holy water', on account of how much it burns. Still makes me wince after all these years."

Liz can't help but smile at the image of an elderly Scottish mime sitting in a backcountry hut knocking back moonshine. A thought occurs to her. "You alone up here?"

The man shrugs. "I'll take that as a no, then?"

"No, sorry." It's now Liz's turn to raise her hands. "Maybe later. I'm just getting my head around..."

"What an old man is doing way out here on his own." The wrinkles etched into the man's face bunch up as he cracks a broad grin.

"Something like that."

"I've walked these trails for years, decades even. The West Coast has a beauty not found anywhere else in New Zealand. You come in from the Lyell end? Bit of a slog wouldn't you say?"

The question is unexpected. Liz fumbles through a response while trying to get her bearings on this place, or more specifically, this man. "Um, yeah... yes. I'm on the mountain bike. I left a bit later than planned. Much later actually. Issues with the cat-sitter."

The man nods thoughtfully for a moment. Then says, "Well, fingers crossed the weather clears tomorrow. Looks like it's just the two of us tonight, then." The wine bottle is placed down on a table closest to the fire and the man pulls out a chair, the legs grinding against the wooden planks of the floor. Before sitting he exclaims, "And where are my manners? The name's Laurence." There is no offer of a handshake, just a welcoming smile, and he lowers himself down onto the chair with a small grunt.

She eyes up the label on the wine bottle; it's faded and worn. The liquid within is clear. She doubts that it's white wine. "Liz."

"Nice to meet you, Liz. So what did you make of Lyell, then?"

"Um, fine. Not much to look at, really." She chooses not to sit, her thoughts are elsewhere: unpacking her bag, getting out of the wet clothes, eating something that isn't an energy bar or trail mix.

"Never used to be that way," Laurence adds, attempting to draw her into conversation.

Liz rises from her daydream. "What's that?"

"Lyell. Used to be a town of about a thousand people. An entire town reduced to a gravel car park full of fancy mobile homes and Lycra'd-up mountain bikers keen to ride the new trail. Oh, er, sorry, no offence. I'm sure those tight-fitting clothes have their place."

"None taken."

Laurence hurries to move the conversation on. "So, er, did you have a read of those information boards dotted around the car park?"

Liz shakes her head. She has a vague memory of several perspex stands housed under slatted, pitched roofs. She paid them little regard thanks to her late arrival to the trail.

"No, you didn't miss much. A bunch of black and white olde-worlde photos and text too small to read. They go on about how Lyell was abandoned when an earthquake struck and fires burned what was left to the ground. Which I guess is technically true, but that's not the whole story."

Laurence fixes her with a mischievous grin, leaning forward with one eyebrow raised. "Of course, they wouldn't want you to know what really happened. Not much of a selling point starting a mountain bike trail at the site of where so many perished. And they called the track The Old Ghost Road. Can you believe that? I guess someone in the marketing department has a dark sense of humour."

The joke is lost on Liz. In any case, her sense of humour was abandoned several kilometres ago when the rain started to fall, saturating her.

"My apologies. You'll have to forgive my ramblings; this holy water has a tendency to loosen my tongue. Please, sit yourself down and dry off. These wooden benches are comfier than they look and your legs must be tired from all that pedalling."

Liz has to admit that he has a point, and the thought of going back out into the elements to sort her bike and gear feels like a weight too heavy to move. She finally succumbs to the offer, relieved to be sitting, but positions herself at the other end of the table. Closer to the flickering flames and also the iron poker resting against the wood burner.

Laurence seems pleased that he now has someone's ear to bend. He swigs from the bottle and winces as the holy water is swallowed down. "... Now, what was I saying?... Ah yes, Lyell. Terrible business. I'm sure you can probably guess why several hundred people moved to the back end of nowhere and called it home?"

"Gold, I'm guessing."

"That's right. You know what the Aztecs used to call it, and excuse my pronunciation—teo-cui-tal-til. Translates as "excrement of the gods". Certainly takes the sheen off that engagement ring you're wearing?"

Liz instinctively makes a fist. It does little to hide the jewellery, but that wasn't her intention. She thinks of the multi-tool again and whether it is less accessible now that she is sat down.

"I'm just messing. It's all right; I'll be on my way once I've polished off this bottle," Laurence says, that mischievous grin returning. "Anyway, in the mid-eighteen hundreds, getting your hands on some of this precious metal would be a golden ticket to a better life. Least, that's what people thought. But for every miner that struck it rich, hundreds toiled away in squalor hoping that with the next swing of the mattock or pan of water their fortunes would change." He smiles to himself as though party to an inside joke. "They came in their dozens at first. That soon turned to hundreds, swarming like sandflies."

The sandfly reference causes Liz to rub several bites on her ankles. The car park had been swarming with them. The insect repellent had done little to protect her from a persistent feature of the West Coast.

Laurence settles himself into a chair, relaxing into the story. "What started as a handful of gold panners squatting in filthy tents evolved into a town with stores, hotels and a post office. They even had themselves a local newspaper. The church had a regular congregation; the pews filled with the faithful in their Sunday best, intently listening to the wise words of the vicar—an ageing man of the cloth who would never be accused of brevity. The dirt road through town bustled with the sounds of horses and carts, and wives congregating in gossiping groups. And if you listened closely, beyond the church choir and the children playing in the streets, it was possible to make out the faint chime of gold being weighed and counted."

The chair creaks as Laurence leans forward, his elbows resting on the table. It's obvious that he's told this story before, the delivery practically scripted. Although still weary, Liz is happy to nod along, the warmth from the fire relaxing her muscles and temperament.

Laurence picks up the wine bottle and gestures towards Liz. "Now, I'd wager the rest of my holy water that the wholesome scene your imagination conjured up doesn't feature a single Maori. Am I right?" Liz isn't given an opportunity to reply before he continues. "'Course I am. But you're actually correct in your racial assumptions, but for the wrong reasons. You see, Maori had already been through these parts. In fact, it was a Maori prospector that first led the Pakeha to the gold seams. One of the few facts those car park information boards got right. Funny that it's not mentioned why it was left to the white man. You don't think it a bit strange that all this potential fortune went untouched?"

Liz doesn't respond, assuming the question is rhetorical; that it's all part of his script.

"Well, maybe it's because Maori people didn't want it. Maybe it was because they knew something that the Pakeha didn't. See, Maori's gold is pounamu— greenstone to you and me. It's found in the depths of Fiordland down south. A place affectionately known as Ata Whenua. You know what that means? Shadowland. Yeah, they've got a flair for the dramatic. Gold, however, that belongs to Whakamomoka, and was not for the taking."

As if in response to saying its name aloud, Laurence takes a deep swig from the bottle. Liz suspects it's more for effect. She thinks over what has just been said. She is familiar with pounamu and Fiordland, but Whakamomoka, that's a new one.

"I'm guessing by your expression you've not heard of Whakamomoka," Laurence says, swishing the liquid around the bottle. "Maybe you know him by his birth name—Rangi. He's an embittered spirit little talked about in Maori folklore. Probably for good reason. He has his origins back when Aotearoa first came into existence - if we're going by Maori mythology - when Maui pulled a great fish out from the sea that eventually became the North Island. The scales of that fish glistened with gold. Captivated by this beauty, Rangi became obsessed and possessive. Anxiety grew within, fearful that the other gods would discover and steal his treasure. These emotions manifested as devastating storms that ravaged the country, felling trees and flooding lands. The gods grew suspicious and soon

Rangi was exposed. He was punished for his weakness. If he loved the gold so much then he would be forever entwined with it. His body and soul were banished into the elements, leaving only his shadow." Laurence's face lights up, relishing the telling of the tale as though addressing a class of school children. But his expression quickly turns grave. "As a final turn of the knife, they smashed up the golden scales and forced them deep down into the fish, forever out of his reach and ensuring that he would never be whole again. Now his shadow drifts through the forests in a kind of purgatory." His tone reverts from excitable storyteller to the conversational delivery of before. "The locals round these parts know him as Whakamomoka, or Stalker, on account of how he seeks out those who carry a small piece of his soul in an attempt to be whole again. The bodies are never recovered. He takes his pound of flesh too."

Laurence takes another swig; the bottle is half-empty. "But back to the gold. The beginnings of this prized metal are a far cry from the finished product. Gleaming trinkets and garish jewellery are in stark contrast to the thick blackness found within the depths of a gold mine. Twelve hours a day those poor miners would labour away in those claustrophobic depths, sucking in the kerosene fumes of the lanterns. A single flickering flame holding back the darkness. Occasionally, shaken miners would emerge, squinting in the sunlight and swearing that there were three of them down there, but four shadows cast across the walls. Maybe it was the effect of the kerosene fumes. Maybe something else was in there with them. Gives me the chills thinking about it."

Liz meets Laurence's stare, noticing that his eyes have become bloodshot. She raises an eyebrow. "Maybe it was too much holy water."

A crack of coarse laughter erupts from Laurence and he nods approvingly. "You know, the offer still stands. Grab yourself a glass."

Liz considers this, knowing that the quicker the bottle is emptied the quicker he may call it a night. But she's not eaten a proper meal since leaving home.

Laurence clears his throat. "Not really selling it, am I? So, where was... ah yes, so it shouldn't come as a surprise that Whakamo... let's stick with Stalker. It shouldn't come as a surprise that Stalker took exception to the pillaging of his gold. With so many involved, in and out of the mines, the intensity of Stalker's anger was unprecedented, measuring 7.8 on the Richter Scale, to be exact." This last detail is delivered with a sense of pride and intellect, before he descends back into drunken rambling. "There's seldom warning when an earthquake hits. And even if there was, what would you do, outrun it? You'd be lucky to manage an unsteady crawl, which was about the best the occupants of Lyell could manage the morning of the seventeenth of June, nineteen-twenty-nine. The ground lurched from side to side, bounded up and down." The wine bottle is waved around like a prop, the contents sloshing within. "Items were shunted off shelves, pictures fell from walls and furniture toppled. However, considering such a violent thrashing, the town remained relatively unscathed. You see, concrete and brick aren't known for their dynamic properties. They'll stubbornly hold their ground and try to fight the shaking. Wood on the other hand, wood will dance and sway, twist and shake." He wiggles back and forth as though to emphasis his point. "It's quite a sight.

Of course the town's vicar decreed that they were all saved by their faith. His jubilant tone was taken down a peg or two when news of the state of the roads in and out of town began to circulate. And when rumours of what occurred at the mines turned to fact, he made himself scarce for several days."

Liz watches Laurence stare long and hard at his drink, his wrinkled fingers wrapped around the bottle. The sound of crackling burning wood competes with the rain lashing against the windows. The weather has worsened. She sighs and is about to politely excuse herself when Laurence pipes back up with a new wave of enthusiasm.

"Locals used to joke that Lyell was the most isolated place in New Zealand. The gods made sure that the gold was scattered far and wide. And as I'm sure you noticed on your ride in, Lyell is surrounded by mountains and forests, boxed in by the Buller River. Well, after the earthquake, jokes about isolation were seldom made. See, there were three ways out of town. The first was an iron bridge across the river. What was left of it resembled a shipwreck lost to the torrent of water it once spanned. Apparently the river ran brown for weeks afterwards due to all the sediment the landslides kicked up. When it mixed with the rust from the fallen bridge it took on a far more ominous tone. The second was via a dirt track that had been cut into the steep hillside. It didn't take much of a nudge for that same hillside to come loose. It tore into the road like an avalanche, wiping it off the map."

Liz thinks this over for a moment. "Didn't you say it was a town of a thousand people? Could they not have dug it out?"

"They could have," Laurence replies, nodding in agreement, "until you consider where most of the able-bodied men were at the time. If you thought those mines were bad enough, now imagine being in the depths of one during a quake. Mine collapse was a common enough occurrence as it was. They used to say that when someone struck it rich, the reason they did not yell out was not because they wanted to avoid alerting others to their fortune, but because of their shoddy working conditions. Kind of like an operatic singer shattering a wine glass. The weight of all that soil would have crushed the very souls of those trapped within. You'd hope that it was quick. I mean... pardon the blasphemy, but Jesus... dries my throat just thinking about it." To remedy this he swallows down another gulp from the bottle and uses it as a pointer, swinging it towards the general direction of Lyell. "You know the bodies are still up there, encased in dirt. They omitted that from those information boards."

Liz dwells on this grim fact for several seconds, knowing that the remainder of the bike ride will be forever tainted. It's as impossible to unhear something as it is to unsee something. She tries to move the conversation on, eager to reach the end of the story. "So what happened then?"

"Exactly a week later - it took that long to build the dozens of coffins, engrave the headstones and dig the graves - the vicar, fresh from his religious retreat, delivered a moving sermon full of vague reassurances.

"The Lord moves in mysterious ways."
"It's all part of His great plan."
"This is a test of your faith."

As Laurence talks he waves his free hand in the air, adding a little flourish with his fingers as though the statements were to be adorned on a theatre billboard. Any sense of entertainment is lost as his tone shifts to a more sombre note. "A mourning heart is a vulnerable thing and widows, fatherless children and the bereaved elderly nodded in agreement as they scattered earth onto empty caskets. If any of them had taken a moment to look up and glance at the trees that ran the length of the cemetery, they would have noticed a silhouette watching and waiting."

"Stalker?" Liz asks, finding herself becoming increasingly engrossed in the tale. Thoughts of unpacking her gear and putting on some food are now secondary concerns.

Laurence nods. He pulls at his scarf and stretches his neck. "Anyway, a stiff southerly wind blew through that day. They say the wailing and sobbing at the funeral could be heard fifty-odd miles away on the coast. And here we arrive at the final nail in Lyell's coffin, if you'll excuse the distasteful pun."

The wine bottle is held up to the light, it's still a quarter full. Laurence considers it with blank curiosity, giving nothing away. He fixes his gaze onto Liz, appearing several years older than when they first met, and asks, "Sure?"

"I'm fine, thanks," she replies through a thin smile.

"Fair enough. If you'll be so kind as to indulge me for a moment."

Liz withholds a sarcastic laugh, but she's too late to stop her eyes rolling. "Of course."

He takes another deep swig, his Adam's apple twitching as he swallows. A hollow pop echoes around the hut when the bottle is removed from his lips and this time Liz struggles to hide a look of distaste. "So... a few months back I met a fellow out walking the Old Ghost

Road. An elderly chap but he wasn't letting his age get the better of him. You know the type: wiry, leathery skin, insists on wearing gators whatever the weather, an improvised walking stick in one hand. It was the gold chain around his neck that caught my eye and led me to spark up conversation. Turns out he used to be a policeman, or a police person, if we're being politically correct about it. In the dog unit, training up German Shepherds to chase down burglars and what not. He owned a dog kennel before that. A doggy daycare sort of thing. He used to swear that a full moon brought out the crazies. At the kennels the dogs would be unruly and unsettled, barking and fighting. Those nights on patrol were always the most hectic, the bright moon enticing the deranged out from under their rocks. Some of the stories he came out with. He showed me bite marks on his forearm and they weren't from the kennels. Now, we have our own kind of full moon here, called the nor'westers."

The unexpected tangent causes Liz to frown. At this rate she'll be here all night.

"They're those dry winds that blow across Canterbury Plains over on the east coast," Laurence clarifies, seemingly picking up on his audience's distraction.

Liz remembers now, the nor'westers start life as westerly gales. As they pass over the mountains their moisture is wrung out, leaving arid winds that whip over the eastern side of the island. "I know the ones," Liz says, "we learnt about them in school."

"I bet they didn't tell you about its grim effects: the spikes in suicide rates and domestic violence? This isn't some new thing either. Maori knew it as Te Hau Kai Tangata." Laurence leans forward in the chair. "Or to you or me - and you'll like this - 'The wind that devours humankind.' Told you they had a flair for the dramatic." He resumes his slouched position in the chair, pleased with himself. "Now if you ask me, the effect it has on people has something to do with that malevolent spirit. The West Coast is predominately forest, meaning that Stalker can move with ease. But the peaks of those mountains that divide the island in two, they rise well above the tree line. And beyond that, there's the vast featureless Canterbury Plains that extend all the way to the sea. Or more specifically, one of the ports where much of his gold was shipped away and turned into shiny jewellery, overpriced watches and dental fillings. I'd hazard a guess that those who are affected by the nor'westers are the same people who are in possession of Stalker's gold." Laurence catches himself and straightens up. "Apologies, I've gone off track a little here. Where was I going with... ah yes, I tell you all this to say that even the weather shouldn't be underestimated out here. There's more than just the rain to be worried about; you don't need to be up on some exposed ridgeline or without waterproofs when the weather turns."

The rain continues to hammer against the hut. Beads of water race down the windows appearing like veins in the glass. Liz thinks about tomorrow's ride—it's a long way to go in the wet. If the weather keeps up she may be forced to retreat back to the car park, or more specifically, back to Lyell. Liz tries to steer him back onto the story. "So, what happened after the funeral?"

It appears that Laurence is also interested in the weather, and he turns from peering out the window to facing her again. "Well, seeing as you're familiar with nor'westers, I take it you are also aware of the southerlies?"

A shiver rattles down Liz's spine. She has plenty of grim memories related to the harsh polar winds that blast through New Zealand on occasion.

"I'll take that as a yes," Laurence says, that crooked grin returning. "So, the town folk were already lighting their household fires now that winter had set in. But no one expected it to last for as long as it did, dragged out by a bitter southerly that blew stronger and longer than anyone could remember. The Antarctic temperatures required the fires to be stoked throughout the day. Ice crept up the window panes once the last flame burned out. And what were once considered ample stacks of firewood were gradually reduced to stumps and off cuts. The depletion of fuel went hand in hand with the depletion of the town's inhabitants. Stories circulated of elderly folk falling asleep in front of a roaring fire, its comforting warmth sending them into a deep and peaceful slumber. And that's where they remained if they didn't wake in time to throw another log on. For the flames didn't just keep the cold away," Laurence points a finger into the air and swirls it around, "but also the shadows. You see, while the rest of the country emerged from a colder than normal winter, Lyell continued to suffer through blizzard-like conditions. Cut off from the rest of the world - with communication and transport links still down - its plight went unnoticed, as one by one the fires burned out."

The unsettling statement causes Liz to inspect the hut's own fire. She swivels around on the bench, collects a log and tosses it in, sending a satisfying burst of embers into the air. She watches the embers settle, then asks, "You're telling me they ran out of firewood? There're acres of forest out there."

"It's not simply a case of taking an axe into the forest and eyeing up a stout tree. Listen to that rain outside. There are places over here that measure rainfall in metres. The forest around Lyell was, is, saturated. It would take a year of summers to dry the place out. The inhabitants of Lyell found that out the hard way, and soon discovered that gold makes for lousy kindling. Imagine it, a widow and her three children gathered around a dying fire. The window panes rattling from the howling wind outside. The cold reach of night creeping ever closer with each smouldering log that's reduced to ash. The mother's gaze darting between the dwindling pile of firewood, the dimming embers, her shivering children and thickening shadows..." Laurence trails off, his gaze fixed on the wine bottle before him. "I mean, God damn." The muttering is barely audible over the lashing rain outside.

Liz says nothing. For the first time since meeting Laurence she feels a sense of pity for the elderly man. It becomes evident that the homemade booze is more of a crutch than a means of passing the cold and lonely nights.

"Now you may be thinking—that rambling drunken fool has forgotten about the third means of leaving town." His gaze does not falter from the bottle, as though it's his sole audience tonight. Liz guesses that on many a night, it is. "I guess now is as good a time as any to get into it. See, there was a miner's track that headed up into the hills. It's the same trail you rode today which brought you to this hut and into my company. Well, if you kept heading north over the Glasgow Range, then you'd eventually arrive at a tiny village called Seddonville. Not an easy trek, especially back in those days, but with the right conditions and enough provisions, doable. However, it was seldom used by the locals. The miners who did brave it, brought back rumours of strange goings-on within the trees, and after what happened to the McGuire twins, the town became convinced that the forest was haunted, cursed, a place that harboured demons. To some degree they were all correct."

Laurence takes a deep breath. He goes to take another swig, but thinks better of it, instead choosing to tightly fold his arms across his chest. The body language unsettles Liz. She shifts in her chair, unsure whether she wants to be party to information that drives a person to drink alone in a backcountry hut.

Laurence clears his throat. "Hannah and Mary McGuire were always considered a mischievous pair. They enjoyed playing tricks on new arrivals to Lyell; the usual twin stuff that teenagers find hilarious, such as dressing the same and appearing to cover impossible distances. They would take it a step further and tie up their long blonde hair under flat caps, smear mud across their freckled faces, adorn matching boys' clothes and continue with the misdirection. The effect on the arrivals was an unsettling feeling that the town was full of child clones.

"The twins were in a group of about ten children who were sent off to collect material to burn, now that firewood was becoming scarce. Fallen branches and the like, stuff not too wet and sodden. While the others preferred to stick to the trail and pick up what they could, the twins thought they could save time and effort by searching the areas off to the side of the track. They had not gone far, maybe less than ten metres, before the forest swallowed them up. While the twins casually added to the piles of sticks within their arms, the vegetation thickened around them, growing at an unnatural rate. The sunlight dimmed, as though eclipsed, and shadows raced through the foliage. Their friends tried to warn them, shouting and yelling, but the cries did not seem to penetrate. Soon the tangle of branches was so thick that it hid the twins from view. And in that moment, everything fell still. For the first time in weeks the trees ceased battling the stiff southerly wind. Forest-dwelling animals hunkered down out of sight. The friends, gathered on the trail, were frozen in fear. There were no screams, no calls for help. Nothing but silence. The kind of silence that precedes the fall of a guillotine blade." The final line is delivered with some satisfaction, as though Laurence has tweaked it over the many retellings of the story.

Liz would have preferred that it was omitted, for it creates the kind of mental imagery she could do without, considering the circumstances.

"The children were not able to say with certainty how long they remained frozen in place," Laurence continues. "Some said a few seconds, others a few minutes. However long it was, at some point they burst from their fixtures and fled back to town. When they returned to the spot with adults at their sides, the wall of tangled branches was absent; nothing like what was described by stuttering, sobbing children. The persistent southerly carried the calls of birds. The only thing of note, discovered by an agitated bloodhound that bayed and snarled, was a mine shaft in roughly the same location that the twins were last seen. It had been abandoned long ago, along with any signage of its presence. It was searched several times, on the assumption that the twins had fallen into its murky depths, but as I mentioned before, bodies are rarely recovered round here."

"Stalker?" Liz asks, her voice a whisper.

Laurence nods slowly. "So another funeral, but this time there were no coffins, no graves - the cemetery was full by this point anyway - just a chunk of rock with the engraved names of Hannah and Mary McGuire. The vicar delivered another sermon, this time from within the protection of the church walls and under the gaze of stained glass windows that had not glowed in months. Once again there were calls for believing in the Great Plan and the mysterious ways of the Lord. The sentiment had been recycled from the countless funerals over the many previous weeks. At some point the tone of the sermon shifted from a belief in faith to a pleading to remain calm. Perhaps it was when the vicar witnessed the shivering congregation eyeing up the thick timber pews, their heads nodding along in feigned interest while they sized up the combustible material. Or maybe it was when he noticed several of them avoiding eye contact, their gaze instead focused on the large wooden cross and life-sized Christ over his shoulder." Laurence's voice becomes more agitated as the list goes on. "Maybe he was aware of the dwindling numbers at Sunday Service and the elderly and infirm absent from the streets. Perhaps he was mindful of the missing bibles with their thin, flammable pages. Or he was dwelling on the previous morning when he woke to discover that the picket fence around the church grounds had been removed. Whatever it was, the pieces all came together to form one conclusion." He looks up at Liz, his eyes unfocused and distant. "Take a moment to revisit that scene of the mother and children gathered around a dying fire. Now picture a wooden crucifix above the mantelpiece. You have to admit, it would make pretty good kindling. I wonder how many turned up to the McGuire funeral having already burned the crucifixes in their homes. How many frames that housed a praying Virgin Mary were torn apart and tossed into the fireplace, the painted canvas soon following?

"Midway through the calls for calm and rationality, a scuffle broke out at the rear of the church—two young mothers fighting over a wooden chair. At first it was thought that they wanted somewhere to sit, but the cause of the dispute quickly became apparent when one of them fled the scene with the chair. Formality and well-to-do-ness shattered. The congregation turned to chaos.

"The vicar tried to intervene. Promising the heathens with damnation if they continued. He would have done better to have thought a little harder when threatening a shivering mob with eternal fire." A smirk creeps across Laurence's face. Liz forces a smile. She's not in the mood for inebriated humour, her patience and politeness wearing thin. "The church was stripped of anything that would feed a flame and, rather ironically, what was left set ablaze. The whole town came out to bathe in the inferno that licked the sky and roared with each blast of frigid wind. Little remained of the church the following morning. The place of worship reduced to the charred logs found in many a fireplace throughout town. No one knew what became of the vicar. No remains were ever recovered."

Liz nods along, her interest now fading. A glance at her watch confirms that it is getting late. Gear needs to be unpacked, food cooked. Although, if she is honest, there is little appetite to please. Liz sits up, pulls her arms in and goes to stand.

"You believe in curses, Liz?" Laurence asks, his words slurred.

Liz lets out a sigh. "Not really." She glances toward the hut door.

Laurence picks up the bottle. Another deep swig. Only a mouthful or two remain. "It began to dawn on the Lyell residents, the ones that hadn't frozen to death, that they may be suffering through a curse of sorts. It's difficult to come to any other conclusion when a plague of rats descends on a town, enticed by the rotting meat of those that were not fortunate enough to have a burial plot. I'm amazed it did not happen sooner. There is many a pest that stalks the forests of New Zealand. Brought over by the colonists, the merciless bastards usually prefer native birds' eggs. Rats, stoats, possums, they've all played their part in killing off the native wild life. But for the days following the church burning, a more tempting feast was laid out. With the inhabitants fearing to go further than a few steps into the surrounding forest, frozen bodies and shallow graves encircled the town. After a few nights the corpses were unearthed and stripped clean, leaving piles of skeletons surrounding those who remained."

"It was only a matter of time before the cold, the isolation and the loss of faith, got the better of Lyell. One by one the buildings of this once prosperous town were torn down for firewood, finishing Stalker's work for him. An unfortunate accident sped up the process." Laurence tips the wine bottle toward Liz and nods as he talks. "With the household fires getting smaller and smaller, and the temperatures dropping, it was to be expected that the inhabitants took to sleeping closer and closer to the flames, hoping to absorb every bit of warmth. All it took was the popping of burning timber for an ember to be cast onto the sheepskin that doubled as a comforting mattress. The singeing woollen fibres soon caught. Woken with a start, the homeowner slung the sheet across the room, landing below a set of heavy curtains. Flames raced up the side of the house and poof!" Laurence splays the fingers of his free hand in another theatrical gesture. "By the time the alarm was raised the fire had already consumed the house and was tearing through the town, travelling with ease through the adjoining buildings. Those caught up in the chaos at least died warm, which was more than could be said for those that subsequently perished from exposure, starvation or diseases associated with eating raw rat meat. The remaining structures suffered the same fate as the church several weeks before. It was almost Christmas by the time the road was cleared from the other side. By then the town was nothing more than charred ruins filled with gorged rats and stripped bones."

Laurence laughs to himself and upturns the bottle over his mouth. Liz watches with relief as the last of the alcohol is drained, relinquishing her from her social responsibilities. She stands and says, "Well, I really should..."

"Now, there's just the one loose end to tie up," Laurence interrupts. The glass bottle is placed back on the table and slid away with his finger tips. "You may be wondering how I came to be in the possession of this knowledge, seeing as the entire town folk perished."

It had not crossed Liz's mind, and she has little interest in finding out. Her only priority is leaving.

Laurence doesn't seem concerned with his guest's intentions and carries on undeterred, untying his scarf in the process. "You see, when I watched my flock turn to savages, and when my pleading for calm and rationality went unheeded, I fell to my knees before that large crucifix and Jesus Christ himself. It was there, hands clasped together and body trembling, I begged for salvation. For our Father to intervene. To spare us. I remained in that position of mercy while the church was stripped bare. The very cross I prayed before was pulled down in front of my eyes. With the suffocating smoke collecting around me, I lost all hope. It was then that he appeared. Not our Father, Jesus or the Dark Lord himself, but Whakamomoka."

Laurence removes the scarf to reveal a clerical collar. Its once-white appearance is faded, almost singed in places. Liz's mouth falls open. She takes two steps back, nearly knocking into the wood burner, the heat from the fire blazing up the backs of her legs.

Laurence remains at the table. His eyes are now sharp and focused and fixed on Liz.

Liz looks to the door. The distance between her and the exit is not far; could be covered in three frantic steps. Her hand is back in her pocket, clenching the multi-tool. The room appears darker, feels darker.

The vicar does not seem concerned with her impending escape and carries on talking. "A great figure loomed over me, darker than the circling smoke, blacker than the depths of a mine. You see, he appears when you are at your most vulnerable, when you're at death's door, when you'll do anything, or agree to anything just to see the light of another day. For you see, a shadow can't interact with the world, can't physically take back what is his."

Liz bolts for the door. Her bike is just outside. It's all downhill to Lyell; she can bear the cold, the rain, the darkness.

The vicar remains seated, unbothered with her escape.

The creaking hinges of the door cry out like sickening laughter as Liz flees into the night. She barely makes it two steps before the sight that awaits her pulls the breath from her lungs. Waiting for her outside are two girls, almost identical in appearance. Their freckled faces are twisted into devious smirks, their once-blonde hair covered with dirt and blood. Stood behind them are several adults. The night shrouds many of their features, but it is possible to make out the mining attire worn by some of the men, and the striped night gowns of the elderly. None of the waiting figures move. They stand like mannequins, rain bouncing off their frozen postures.

A trembling hand covering her mouth, Liz stumbles back and collides with the door frame. The multi-tool slips from her fingers onto the sodden ground.

"Best come in from the rain before you catch a death," Laurence says from inside the hut. "Besides, we need to have a chat about those gold fillings of yours. You really should have accepted that drink, it helps numb the pain."

Author's Note

The more short stories I have written, the more I have enjoyed writing them.

Many of these tales started life as submissions for podcasts, usually based around a specified theme and word count. It is these restrictions that inadvertently influenced my writing style. When you're up against a word count, the superfluous descriptions and drawn-out content need to be streamlined. As a result, I've found it's more effective to let the reader do the work. Nothing I write will be scarier or as unsettling as an individual's imagination. The result is a story personalised to each reader, with an ending that lingers in the back of their mind for the rest of the day while they fill in the dark and murky blanks. At least, that is the hope.

So if you would like to support an aspiring indie author, then please consider leaving a review. This simple gesture goes a long way in the self-publishing world and encourages others to spend some of their days filling in their own dark and murky blanks.

Head over to www.ianjmiddleton.com for two exclusive short stories:

The devil's in the detail.

It was meant to be an easy placement for Constable Ralph Jackson, trading the hustle and bustle of city policing for the slow beat of village life. It would be a chance to put his feet up for a few months, tick an experience box, and edge his career another rung up the ladder.

However, his expectations are immediately tarnished when he is assigned to two missing person cases. As he struggles to adapt to a slower pace of life, he begins to unearth something sinister that lurks below the surface of this sleepy mountain village.

While attempting to connect the dots, he acts on a hunch that leads him to confront an unexpected suspect in the hope of solving the mystery before the culprit strikes again.

A dark and unsettling installment to Vantage Point lore that will play on your mind long after the paint has dried.

Exhausted from unproductive meetings, worried about a failing marriage and desperate for somewhere to lay his head for the night, The Vantage Point Hotel should have been a stroke of good fortune.

But things are never what they seem in the sleepy alpine village.

Whether it's the unruly guests, neglectful customer service or that lingering feeling that something isn't quite right, all the signs point to an unsettling realisation in this haunting short story.

Available at: www.ianjmiddleton.com

About the Author

Ian J. Middleton is originally from Cardiff, Wales, but now lives with his partner, two sons and two dogs in Christchurch, New Zealand.

When he is not attending to his many responsibilities, he may be found either at a keyboard or on a mountain bike with a (sometimes sinister) smile on his face.

Ian may be found on:

Email: hello@ianjmiddleton.com

Website: www.ianjmiddleton.com

Instagram: @ianjmiddleton